CW00841127

About the Author

I write books and I make games. In the event that Sofa Space doesn't immediately make you want to jettison me out of a conveniently placed spaceship airlock, you can find out about more of my projects on my website:
http://www.tomcheshire.com

I'd like to dedicate Sofa Space to my family, my friends and that one weird dream I had about caffeine and robots.

1

Imagine the worst hangover of all time. You know the pain, when it feels like your head is on fire? Imagine that, only twice as bad. Now combine it with the fatigue of being locked in a prison cell for a couple of decades. Losing all sense of self, forgetting what it feels like to be alive. Having no concept of who, where, what, why or how, but knowing for certain that something must have gone incredibly wrong at some point to end up in such a sorry state. This was going to be one of those days...

I'd woken up. Where? I wasn't entirely sure. Having fumbled around for a non-existent alarm clock, I eventually realised that waving my arms in the air was a rather fruitless exercise, so I let my arms go limp, and... ah... that's strange. My arms made contact with rounded metal accompanied by a comically audible 'thump,' and instantly I knew that this wasn't my bed. Hell, this didn't feel like any bed I'd laid in before. I let my arms slide along the surface, the metal curving cylindrically either side. Was this some kind of medical device? Hard to tell; my arms were extremely numb and hardly even in sync with my thoughts. From what little sensory input I had, I was able to deduce that whatever I was lying in was extremely narrow, and probably not all too comfortable for the downstairs region.

Had I been in some kind of accident? What was that burning pain? After spending a few moments clarifying that my head was not actually on fire, I tried to move my legs but my lower body hadn't woken up. Give it a minute, I thought. I tried to open my eyes - big mistake. The resultant flash of light penetrated my poor unsuspecting retinas. In its wake, a lingering afterimage danced, mockingly, across my eyelids, continuing long after the instinctual reaction to shut both eyes as quickly as humanly possible.

Minutes passed and I began to suspect that whatever had caused the piercingly bright light was, in fact, nothing out of the ordinary, that I'd just been out of it for so long my eyes had forgotten to adjust. Just a bit of sunlight creeping through the window, surely? Slowly I eased my eyes into a narrow gaze, locked in an odd-looking position of perpetual squinting until I could finally make out something vaguely resembling a ceiling. Grey? Definitely grey, I thought. That or my eyesight had deteriorated to the point of rendering everything in monochrome.

Slowly but surely my other senses returned to me. There was a faint whirring sound that seemed to be reverberating all around me. The cool air smelled of a certain freshness that was probably supposed to be welcoming but… hang on, was that coffee? Delighted that I had apparently recovered my senses enough in order to correctly identify the scent of coffee, I began floundering my limbs around like an idiot, trying to find a way to force my body up and out of whatever I was in. Yes, time to get up, lazy boy. Can't lie here forever. A few seconds later my head had introduced itself to the floor and I immediately regretted that train of thought.

"Damn that coffee!" I swore aloud, although my lack of muscular control reduced those words to meaningless grunts. It seemed odd to blame the coffee for my current predicament, but I couldn't think of anything else to use as a scapegoat. I'm not sure how long I stayed face-down on the floor, but it was long enough to induce a whole new set of aches and pains by the time I rolled over.

Finally I was able to stand. That coffee again… it was still there; the scent was much stronger now. The deliciously caffeinated aura filled my nostrils, guiding me forwards. I was nowhere near balanced, stumbling around like an intoxicated fool. I found myself slamming into pipes and walls and pieces of equipment I couldn't identify. Everything was just an indistinct haze at this point - the coffee was the only thing I could focus on. My whole brain was preoccupied by the goal of reaching it; I wasn't even paying attention to where I was. I followed my nose and limped through some sort of corridor until I could start to hear voices. Voices! That should have been cause for me to forget about my blind-sighted objective, but it wasn't. I tripped through a doorway vaguely aware of four agape faces staring back at me. I took a few more steps in the general direction of the coffee scent until my legs gave way. I suppose I passed out a few moments later. Oh well, it was worth a shot.

"That's why I thought he was dead!" was the first sentence I caught as I returned to consciousness.

"Thought who was dead?" I yawned, groggily. As I rubbed my eyes I got the sense that several people quickly shuffled away from me, alarmed at my sudden awakening. I sure as hell hoped they hadn't been trying to revive me through some form of close bodily contact.

"You, obviously!" came the first voice again. I turned my head towards the source, spending a few moments trying to determine if I knew who it was. I quickly realised that was too much effort, and focused on just examining features. Facing me was a slightly overweight man, probably in his early 30s, wearing a baggy shirt and jeans, leaning on a burgundy-coloured sofa at a slightly awkward angle. His ginger hair was long and looked pretty unkempt, curling off in random directions. He also had a silly looking goatee - still ginger, but with a mismatched hue compared to the rest of his hair. Instantly I could tell that he was in a bad mood.

"Well, no. I'm not dead," I said. The ginger man turned away, as if trying to think of some clever remark to bark back with.

"You stopped breathing," came a woman's voice. "Are you sure you feel alright?"

How my declaration of not being dead had somehow implied that I was feeling alright, I did not know. I turned to the woman planning to say something sarcastic about my head being on fire, but her face seemed genuinely sympathetic, so instead I was honest.

"I've got a hell of a migraine. What's going on?"

The ginger man did a fake-sounding chuckle, as if that was a stupid question. The woman looked down at the floor, dark hair flowing across her face, which she brushed out of the way incredibly slowly, giving herself time to think. She was pretty, I suppose, or perhaps the unkempt ginger man had been such an eyesore that I was ready to accept almost anyone else. The stripy, charity shop-esque jumper she was wearing certainly wasn't doing her any favours.

"We don't know what's going on either, but we've been awake for a little longer than you have. We think..." she paused. "We think we're on a spaceship."

"What?" I gasped, suddenly taking in my surroundings. It didn't look much like I'd expect a spaceship to look; there were a few pipes and odd metallic bits and pieces, but from what I could tell we were in an ordinary-ish 21st century living room. There was the sofa the ginger man was leaning on alongside a coffee table, a couple of empty bookshelves and a large monitor that I assumed was a TV.

"Are you pulling my leg?" I asked. "Is this some kind of practical joke? It's not a very good one. You haven't exactly gone to town on the set design..."

There was an awkward pause. I tried again.

"Seriously? Is this a joke?"

"Afraid not," came a different woman's voice. She was wearing glasses and a smart black dress with her hair tied up in a neat bun, suggesting a sort of authoritative confidence I couldn't see in the others. "This is just the common room. I think it's supposed to look like Earth, to make us feel at home."

"Yeah, feels real homely don't it..." came the ginger man's sarcastic tone.

"Okay, fine, how did I get here?" I asked, smirking in disbelief.

"You came in through that doorway and collapsed. Started muttering something about coffee…" replied the ginger man.

"I meant how did I end up on a bloody spaceship?" I asked, getting frustrated. I knew it wasn't really a spaceship but I thought we'd get to the point quicker if I played along. Being reminded of that damn coffee didn't help.

"Um…" came a new voice, which startled me because I'd forgotten there was another person in the room. I turned around to see an older, timid looking man, probably in his 60s, with greying hair and a tattered white shirt. He had a somewhat awkward demeanour. "There's… c..cryo pods…" he mumbled, stammering slightly.

I followed the others through a slightly more convincingly spaceship-like corridor back to the room where I'd first woken up. The older man was right, this was a room filled with cryogenic pods. By which I mean, things that looked like cryogenic pods, but couldn't possibly be cryogenic pods because that's stupid. Still, I couldn't knock the authenticity of the design. They were human-sized cylindrical chambers with glass windows coated in a thick layer of condensation, connected to some sort of large vat reinforced with steel. Anyone who's ever seen a science fiction film before would have guessed they were cryogenic pods from just a quick glance.

"But… this doesn't explain anything." I said, still going along with this prank. "Who put me in there? Why can't I remember?"

"We've all got this amnesia," said the confident girl. "It must be a side effect from being frozen for so long."

"So long? What do you mean, so long?" I asked, ignoring what the words 'cryogenically frozen' implied. The ginger man pointed towards a small numerical dial on the top of one of the pods.

"25 years, every single one of them," he said, bitterly. "We've been asleep for a quarter of a century."

That was a funny old premise, being asleep for so long. Let's think about this for a moment. 25 years. What would it mean to lose out on such a long amount of time? All the important stuff I would have missed back home... What about my parents? What was the last thing I said to my wife? My kids? Would they even be alive? Wait a second; did I even have a wife? Hang on a minute. There's something really wrong here... That's when I realised.

"I don't remember my family..." I said, softly. "I... I don't remember my name." It was true, and the fact that I had only just realised was petrifying. I was straining myself to remember these basic details but the only picture I could paint was blank. This prank was getting more and more sinister by the second. "What the hell did you guys do to me? Have I been drugged? Tell me what's going on!" Before I knew it I had an arm round me. It was the dark haired girl.

"I'm sorry..."

"It doesn't make any sense!" I yelled. It wasn't like I'd had my memory completely wiped, because surely I'd have woken up having forgotten how to speak and spent all morning crying and rolling around on the floor like a newborn child. On second thoughts that wasn't far from the truth, but that's besides the point. I couldn't remember who I was, or what I did for a living, yet somehow I knew in my heart that I'd lived a productive life. I must have. The Beatles, Jackie Chan, Super Mario. Every now and then a pop culture reference would flicker annoyingly into my head, and hell, I recognised the smell of coffee, so clearly not everything had been wiped.

"Alright, that's enough..." I said calmly. "The joke's getting tired now, guys, this isn't funny."

"Now now, let's not start thinking irrationally," said the confident girl. "Nobody drugged you. It's just a bit of cryogenic amnesia, we've all got it. Something must have gone wrong with the process. None of us can remember our families or our names at the moment..."

"And I'm supposed to believe that, am I?" I responded.

"Look, take all the time you need, but please just trust me. We'll all on the same page here," she replied.

"It's true. I don't know who I am, either," the other girl said despondently. The tone of her voice was genuine.

If that was supposed to make me feel better, it wasn't very effective. The ginger man sensed this, and decided to make the most of this opportunity to wind everyone up.

"My name's Dom, I've got a wife and family in Texas. I'm 33 years old and I drive trucks for a living," he stated, grinning idiotically. It was obviously complete bullshit, and not just because his accent was clearly British.

"You're l… lying," stammered the old man, eyes down at the floor.

"No sh… shit of course I don't remember who I am!" yelled the ginger man, his imitation of the old man's stammer causing a ripple of disapproval among the others. "Not only that, I didn't even remember which gender I was this morning until I looked down and was like, woah, dude, what's that dangling between my legs? It's huge! I mean we're talking about morning wood 25 years in the making right here…"

Stunned silence.

"Oh come on!" he continued. "You don't honestly believe this horse shit do you? 25 years, my arse. Look, guys, we can cry all we want, but whatever's happened to us, someone's obviously responsible. Let's not jump to bullshit sci-fi conclusions." Finally someone was starting to talk some sense.

"Ginger guy has a point…" I said. Ginger guy seemed to take offense.

"Really? Ginger guy? Wow, okay. We're gonna resort to adjectives now? Male pattern baldness…"

I nervously started feeling around for my hairline.

"We can't just sit around here for days waiting to remember who we bloody are. We're gonna have to come up with names for ourselves."

The confident girl started pacing up and down, trying to gauge the right moment to say something.

"I hate to say it…" she started. "But he's right. We don't know how long this amnesia will last. We have to find some way to identify ourselves." The old man glanced up, finally, as if he was about to say something, but chose not to. The confident girl continued. "Feels like we've gotten off to a bad start. I think we should all have some time alone… Choose a name, and we'll meet back later on to introduce ourselves, yeah?"

Nobody was in the mood to question her logic. We walked back through the corridor and stood in separate corners of the common room. There was a distinct lack of furniture to actually sit on other than the sofa that nobody seemed brave enough to try out. What followed was an increasingly tense hour or so of complete silence, during which we each tried to avoid making eye contact with everyone else. Well, apart from the ginger man, who took great pleasure in walking around being as deliberately distracting as possible without actually saying anything.

Eventually the tension was too much to bear so I chose a doorway at random and started walking. From what I could deduce, the actual living space of this "spaceship" we were on was rather small indeed, consisting mainly of the central common room with multiple exits and a single corridor that wrapped around in a sort of horseshoe shape. There were doors to the 'cryo room', a couple of smaller, featureless rooms that I assumed were supposed to be bedrooms (minus the beds), a bathroom and a door that wouldn't open, not that I was trying very hard to open it. Despite the ever-twisting pipes and railings in the corridor, nothing on this 'spaceship' looked very sophisticated to me. The doors were all on hinges and had physical handles, and not even the clean, modern sort. I'm talking tacky, half-rusted brass handles that were so stiff you could hardly turn them. Certainly not the sort of thing Captain Kirk ever had to put up with. There's another reference for you. I'd have congratulated myself on the ability to recall another element of popular culture, but the thought of William Shatner being one of the only faces left in my memory was demoralising, so I let it pass.

Before long, I found myself in the bathroom, transfixed by my own reflection in the mirror. I felt a certain sense of recognition, but not a clear one. The ginger man was right, my hairline was receding. Well, that's great, I thought, unsure whether I should laugh or cry. I went for the latter, because it seemed to be the normal reaction to being told you've been frozen for 25 years with no memories of your former life. No, that's still stupid, I thought. I wasn't ready to start believing that crazy story just yet.

Before long I found myself daydreaming, trying to invent my own past history in order to justify the ridiculous setting I found myself in. I started to figure that if everything the others were saying was true, as ridiculous as it may seem, maybe there was some logic behind it. Maybe we were all astronauts on some experimental mission to explore the deepest regions of space, and like the confident girl had said, something went wrong with the freezing process resulting in us losing our memories. No, that does sounds bonkers. Space astronauts? Cryogenic freezing? How could any of it be true? And further still, would I really commit to a career like that? I didn't fancy myself as much of a spaceman. Maybe a banker or accountant or something really boring like that. But what did I know? I could have been a convicted criminal. Maybe this was some kind of mental asylum. I shuddered with the thoughts of things I could have done in my earlier life to deserve this.

I still had to choose a name. Jack? Sam? Paul? Mark? I glanced up at my pathetic tear stained face. Guess I was just your average…

2

"Joe? That's the best you've got?" asked the ginger man, doing his best to make me resent my newly chosen identity.

"Uh… yeah, there a problem with that?" I responded.

"No, no… just… never mind."

"Why did you stick with the name Dom?"

"It's easy to remember."

"Well there you go."

The dark haired girl had chosen the name Emma, while the confident girl was extremely confident that her name was Chloe and 'couldn't possibly be anything else' no matter how much Dom pushed her. That left the old man, whom when pressured for a name couldn't come up with anything so Dom gave him the name Travis. Because it made him laugh.

So, there in the common room we stood, five complete would-be strangers with fake identities introducing ourselves like a group of students on freshers' week, discussing fake details of our fake lives as if any of us had a clue what we were talking about. None of us stopped to question what we were doing, because there was something oddly cathartic about being able to make up details of our past lives without feeling any guilt about lying. Before the end of our conversation I had become an engineer, Emma a teacher, Chloe an investment banker and Travis (after much prodding by Dom) an artist. Dom changed his mind about his backstory and instead gave us an elaborately constructed tale of how he was the 'top dog' of a world renowned 'pimping agency,' owned a whole chain of strip clubs and was 'banging thirty hoes' a week, because 'wouldn't that be awesome?' 'Dom the Schlong,' he called himself. Suffice to say he really enjoyed fleshing out that story, while Chloe and Emma were horrified.

On the whole though, I began to warm to the group. Part of this was undoubtedly tactical, as in: 'I don't know how long I'll be stuck with these folks so I better bloody get on with them.' Part of it must have been genuine, however. None of the people were grating on me yet, not even Dom, whose cocky arrogance had somehow swung so far into the realms of tastelessness that it had almost become charming. I'd zoned out. Dom was still going on about his pimping business and Chloe and Emma were having a jokey argument with him about the morals of prostitution. I groaned.

"What is it, Joe?" Emma asked.

"What are we doing?" I sighed. "Let's look at the facts. We're stuck on a spaceship."

"Supposedly," interjected Dom.

"We don't know why we're stuck on a spaceship-"

"Supposedly..."

"And instead of trying to find out why we're stuck on a spaceship-"

"Supposedly..."

"We're sitting around talking about 12 inch dildos."

"Human nature," Dom shrugged. Yeah, human nature, or had we already lost our marbles?

"How come..." I began, trying to come up with an observation as I spoke, "...we're all wearing casual clothes? I mean shouldn't we all be wearing space uniforms or something? If we're really in space..."

"That's right," said Travis, who hadn't said much throughout the whole conversation. "It's kind of... o... odd, isn't it?"

"Well we woke up in them, so who knows," replied Emma. "Obviously doesn't do any harm to the cryo pods."

"That's weird," Chloe pondered. "Must be a new type of cryogenic-"

"Do you know something we don't?" Dom snapped. "Because the last time I checked, cryogenic pods in space were the stuff of bleeding sci-fi!"

"When was the last time you checked?"

"It's a figure of speech!"

"Well for your information, Dom the self-proclaimed pimp…"

"Dom the Schlong." Dom corrected her.

"Right, Dom the Schlong, I think you'll find they've been doing cryogenic freezing tests for years in labs and such," Chloe paused. "I think."

"Yeah but not in space," Dom retorted. "God knows what year it is now, but I remember the turn of the millennium like it was yesterday. We're from the early twenty-first century! This shit doesn't exist!"

That nobody piped up after this comment implied that we were all indeed from the same time period, which as Dom stated, must have been some time in the early twenty first century. Maybe. Putting aside the amnesia for one moment, it was almost impossible to recall definitive dates after half an hour of irreverent strip club discussion.

"So let's see here," I began. "We've woken up with no memories wearing non-futuristic clothes and we're in a non-futuristic looking room with a sofa and goddamn doors with brass handles. And that means we're in space. Why?"

"Have you looked out the window yet, Joe?" Chloe said, as if I was being stupid.

"No," I replied, dumbfounded. "What window?"

I followed Chloe's eyes over to the large rectangular black object I had previously assumed was a TV. As I got closer, my jaw hung wide as it suddenly dawned on me that I'd missed something obvious. There were no stars, maybe one or two max, but somehow my brain knew instantly that I was looking out into deep space. The same way that when you look up at the night sky, even when there's nothing visible, you get a sensation of openness, of vastness. Standing here, looking horizontally out at the great black nothingness I got a sense of vertigo. I suppose it's a natural feeling. You're used to seeing space as this thing above your head, not in front of it.

"Wow," was the only thing I could say. I glanced towards the edges of the window and could just make out some of the exterior of the ship, a textured grey that appeared to extend outwards at perfectly straight angles. I got the impression that the ship was shaped like a box. A big grey box drifting alone in a much bigger black ocean. The exterior was casting some kind of light somehow, as there certainly wasn't a nearby sun shining our way. I wasn't going to even begin to contemplate where all the power was coming from.

"Do you believe me now?" Chloe asked, wearing her best 'I told you so' face.

"Yeah, I think so," I said, wanting to just keep staring out into the emptiness.

"Seriously?" Dom huffed. "You think they can build a spaceship with goddamn cryogenic freezing pods, but they can't build, say, a 3D monitor with a bit of snappy head tracking? You know, like the stuff that already exists…"

"You seriously think someone would go out of their way to fake this?" Emma asked, joining in with the debate.

"It's a lot more believable than some of the shit you guys are coming up with! Jesus, I thought you'd have gotten the hint after my pimping story. Everything here is bullshit. Someone's playing us."

"Playing us?"

"Yes, Emma, playing us. I'm telling you, we're being watched." Dom started shifting his eyes around the room suspiciously. "You guys want to know my theory?"

Nobody said anything, but we let him continue.

"I think we're on some kind of crazy reality TV show. Japanese, I'll bet. They probably gave us some pills to make us forget everything, then they put us in those tacky pods and started rolling the cameras." Dom started imitating a reality show announcer voice. "Five contestants wake up with no memories. They think they're on a spaceship. Which one of them will lose their mind first? Find out on next week's episode of Numpties in Space!"

Dom was really getting into his mad little piece of role play, as he started humming a silly made up theme tune and running around like a five year old impersonating an astronaut. The rest of us shook our heads.

"Dom, would you cut it out?" Chloe asked.

"Why should I? This is the stuff that brings in the ratings," Dom smiled, "They'll be lapping this up, the public. Ginger twat goes crazy and rumbles reality show on day one! Think of the headlines," he started laughing maniacally. "BIG BROTHER! I'M A GINGER TWAT GET ME OUT OF HERE!"

Again, more pop culture references I didn't particularly want to recall at this moment in time.

"THERE YOU GO! I'VE RUMBLED YOU! YOU CAN KICK ME OUT NOW! SHOW'S OVER!" Dom continued yelling with glee. Chloe and Emma both covered their ears.

"Must be a way out, it's only a TV set after all…" Dom continued, combing the room for secret exits. He started tapping on one of the walls. "Let's see how well they built it." Dom started banging on the wall, lightly at first, but gradually harder and harder until he was punching with all his strength.

"Dom, please stop punching the wall…" Chloe sighed.

"Right, okay, guess they did a pretty good job. YOU HEAR THAT, MR. PRODUCER? YOU BUILT A DAMN GOOD SET!" Dom stopped pounding on the wall and began nursing his hand. I wouldn't have been surprised if he'd busted a few bones.

"There's blood on the wall now," he said, softly, but with an aura of pride. "I should sue them for that." I glanced over to the spot on the wall Dom had been punching. There was a small sprinkling of red, but other than that, not a mark in sight. Whatever these walls were made of, it would take something a lot stronger than Dom's fist to make a dent in them.

For a short moment, we thought Dom had calmed down. Chloe and Emma sat down on the sofa, Travis resumed his default state of 'looking at the floor,' and I continued to gaze thoughtfully out of the window. Before long, however, it was clear Dom had other plans. He slowly turned his eyes in my direction, stared at the window and smiled triumphantly. Then he walked over to the coffee table and tried to pick it up. It wouldn't budge.

"Huh… Seems to be fused to the floor. Okay then, I'll have to use something else…" Dom looked up at Chloe and Emma. "Excuse me ladies," he said calmly. It was clear that he wasn't asking to sit down, as there was plenty of room on the sofa. Instantly I clocked on to what he was trying to do.

"No… you can't," I warned.

"Shut up, Joe! Ladies, would you mind?" He was gesturing for them to stand up. Emma moved right away, but Chloe remained seated. "Chloe just stand up for one sec."

"No."

"Chloe, please."

"No!"

By this point Dom was practically wrestling Chloe out of the sofa. Travis suddenly stepped into action.

"Stop it Dom! Let her s…sit!"

"I'm getting us out of here, Travis, if you people would… just… co-operate!" Dom finally managed to force Chloe out of her seat. She looked back at him, eyes filled with fury. Dom clearly didn't care, as he was too busy trying to pick the sofa up.

"Dom, what the hell are you doing?" Emma asked, agitated.

"Getting… hnnnghh!!... out!" The huge sofa was clearly much heavier than Dom had predicted, but before long he had started to lift it. The floor underneath was surprisingly spotless.

"Dom! Oh my god!" Emma yelled, then placed her hands over her mouth in shock. Dom half-dragged the sofa over towards the window, and I rushed to the other end trying to push it back.

"Joe, would you please let me do this!" Dom shouted.

"If you smash that window, we'll all die!" I yelled. "We'll be sucked into the vacuum of space!"

"We're not in fucking space!"

I looked to the others for help, but Emma was crying, Chloe was in a sort of hate-fuelled trance and Travis was cowering in the corner. Dom's strength was unfortunately much greater than mine, and I fell to the ground, hitting my head on the coffee table.

"It's the only way!" Dom screamed, as he lifted the sofa as high as he could, and launched it towards the window with all his might.

"NOOOO!!!"

In the few milliseconds before the impact, I somehow had enough time to mentally contemplate several potential scenarios. One, that the window would be strong enough to withstand a direct collision, the sofa rebounding and landing squarely on Dom, perhaps killing him or at least incapacitating him to the point where he would never try something so stupid again. Two, that the sofa would go flying straight through the window, thus creating a hole into space, immediately sucking all of us out with the pressure and killing us all. Three, that Dom was actually right, the window really was a fake all along and that after smashing through it we'd be greeted by a film production crew wearing headphones, sitting around with video monitors and clipboards. I found myself greatly preferring scenario number one. Even though three would technically put an end to this nightmare, in the end of the day I just couldn't stand to see Dom victorious.

Actually, all three of these scenarios were wrong. As the sofa collided with the window it smashed straight through, but before the vacuum of space began to take its toll, a blue flash of light appeared where the window once was and the glass magically repaired itself. No broken glass on the floor, no damage at all. The sofa, however, carried on its trajectory, very slowly rotating its way out into space. All five of us watched in silence as it gradually span into the distance, slipping further and further away. We continued to watch it glide out of reach for what must have been several minutes. Chloe sighed.

"Now we've got nowhere to sit, asshole!"

3

The lack of seating didn't exactly help group morale. Perhaps we were overreacting. I gazed out at the sofa, now but a tiny gyrating cuboid, trying to imagine how we'd all have managed to sit together. I quickly came to the conclusion that it wasn't possible for all five of us to perch upon it at the same time, although with a bit of effort we might have been able to squeeze on four. The sofa had only been a double seater, but the girls and I were slim enough to have easily sat together without brutally violating each other's personal space in the process. Travis could have climbed up onto the armrest, though it would have probably been a bit uncomfortable for his old bones. Dom? No combination of body positions would have allowed for his bulky frame to fit on there too, I decided, picturing the disturbing image of a collapsed sofa with human limbs protruding outwards in all directions. It might be possible to fit a couple of dozen people in a Mini, but as far as comfortable seating arrangements go, I wouldn't exactly call it practical.

I bring this up because for a considerable amount of time after Dom's little outburst, all that the others and I could think about was that bloody sofa, as if having something pleasant to sit on was the be-all-end-all solution to all our problems. Yeah, it does seem silly, but perhaps it was the manner in which the damn thing was still just about visible to the naked eye. Every time the cosmic couch rotated fully on its axis it would catch the light coming from the ship, reminding us that it was still there, just out of arm's reach, taunting us with its soft plush burgundy cushions that would now go untouched for millions of years.

But yeah, we were overreacting. The floor of the common room had a soft, textured feel to it that was fine for sitting on, probably even passable enough as a last-resort sleeping location. The empty bookshelves in the corners of the room were rather pleasingly rounded and fine for leaning on, probably even fine for lying down on. The coffee table was just about high enough for people to sit on without it a) breaking or b) putting an unnatural strain on the pelvic muscles. Nevertheless, we weren't happy.

Travis sensed this, and, perhaps out of fear of some future explosive incident, proved himself to be quite adept in coming up with solutions to our seating predicament. He fused a few plastic sheets and loose pipes together to make something vaguely resembling an armchair, and quickly fashioned up a couple more. For something so obviously hacked together, I was surprised to find that it actually wasn't all that bad to sit on. He claimed he got all the materials from rummaging around in the walls of the ship's corridor, but honestly I have no idea how he managed to build it all so quick. I hadn't even thought about looking through the ship's innards (there were metal gratings all over the corridor holding all kinds of bits and bobs) because I didn't have a clue what any of it was; I figured I might accidentally blow up the ship in the process. Perhaps I'd been a technophobe in the past. As long as Travis knew what to do, that was fine by me.

I wasn't in a position to suspect Travis was some kind of imposter or anything like that. He'd certainly been the quietest and most reserved member of the group so far, but his age was quite telling. This was a man who'd been around long enough to know how to knock something together from spare parts, and we were very grateful to have someone like that with us, even if we couldn't quite admit it.

"Thanks Travis," I said, slumped on one of his improvised chairs and trying to sound sincere, although something about the name Travis didn't seem to lend itself well to compliments. Travis made an odd nervous squeak of acknowledgement, then sat down on the floor. This was odd, because one of his makeshift creations was unoccupied, and neither Dom nor Chloe (who were both standing up, arms crossed, having said nothing since the sofa incident) looked like they wanted to try it out.

"You sure you don't want to take a seat?" I asked tentatively.

"Nah… nah..." Travis mumbled, shaking his head and looking at the floor. I waited a few moments before launching into another half-arsed compliment.

"It's good, this," I said, rubbing my hands along the angular armrests. "Very comfy."

"O...oh… I'm glad." Travis smiled weakly.

"You must be tired after all that work. Why don't you try it out?"

"I'm good."

That was all I was going to get out of him, clearly. I could have taken the Dom approach and forced him to sit in the chair but I didn't want to start getting aggressive, especially after all the drama from earlier.

Not long after this little exchange, Chloe decided she was going to sit down in the unoccupied chair. I'm guessing it was to make sure Dom didn't get there first, although he was never going to make a move. I highly doubt he was in the mood to damage his reputation any further. Once Chloe had gotten settled, I tried to get a conversation going.

"You alright, Chloe?"

Instead of looking towards me, Chloe turned in completely the opposite direction, resting her hand under her chin. Not a good time to chat, clearly. Travis shot me a look as if to say 'let's just sit here keeping ourselves to ourselves.'

Actually, no. I was starting to feel light-headed. I wasn't in the mood to sit for another few minutes in dead silence. I needed to talk to someone before I collapsed out of sheer boredom. I figured I'd have more success if I tried with Emma.

"Hey Emma."

"Hey…"

"You alright?"

"Yeah…"

It was one of those automatic 'yeahs' that is always the default response to being asked if you're alright, even when you're clearly not.

"Good good…" Well, great. There goes another potential conversation. Why did I have to ask such a stupid question? Guess I'd have to shut up now, before things got any more awkward.

"Joe?" Emma asked.

"Yeah?"

"You're bleeding."

And so I was. Well, that explained my light-headedness. I put my hands to my face and found that I had a gash on my forehead.

"Must have been when I fell and hit that coffee table."

Coffee table. Saying those words out loud finally reminded me of something.

"Damn coffee," I muttered to myself.

"What's that about coffee?" asked Chloe, suddenly alert.

"Nothing. Coffee table. I hit the coffee table, that's why I…"

"No, you kept going on about coffee earlier, back when you passed out."

"Did I?" I tried to pretend that I couldn't remember.

"Yeah, it was, like, the only thing you kept saying. Damn coffee, over and over again."

"That's weird."

I suddenly found that Emma was handing me some paper towels. She must have grabbed them from the bathroom. I held them up to my forehead. I wasn't bleeding heavily, but it was enough to put everyone off.

"You scared us," Emma said. I assumed she was talking about my subconscious coffee ramblings, and not the bloody mess on my forehead.

"I'm sorry about that," I said. "So whose coffee was it, anyways? Could sure use one about now."

Everyone stared at me like I was slipping back into unconsciousness, but I was pretty sure, despite the blood loss, that I was feeling fine.

"Joe… there was no coffee." Emma said delicately.

"But I could smell it..."

"Joe, there was no coffee." Chloe repeated Emma's words with a stricter tone.

"There must have been. It's what woke me up!"

"Joe!"

"It was so strong, it must have been real!"

"Joe, snap out of it!" It was Dom, finally speaking after the whole sofa incident. I suddenly felt very small. It was like the tables had turned; now all of a sudden I was the crazy one. The others were starting to look at me as if I was dangerous, as if my steadfast belief that I'd smelt coffee this morning was the first step towards becoming a serial killer.

"I just thought I could smell coffee, that's all!" I half-shouted, standing up and darting out of the common room, hand still supporting my head wound. I wanted to get away from everyone.

I stood in the bathroom, staring at my reflection yet not thinking about my injury. Instead I was putting all my effort into focusing on my senses. Was it really possible that I'd imagined the whole coffee thing?

It's funny. Waking up with no memories of my former life, so far I'd found that my senses were the only thing I had absolute trust in. Everything was mental, but I didn't doubt that what had happened in front of me had been real. The sight of the great burgundy sofa colliding with the self-repairing glass. The rough feel of the angular metal armrests on Travis' almost-chairs. The faint whirring sound from the cryogenic pods, reverberating through all the walls of the ship. My brain was telling me that these things were ridiculous, I mean for Christ's sake, waking up in space! How the hell do you even begin to rationalise that? The only way I could was to trust what my senses were telling me. No, this wasn't a dream. This was happening here, now. A cut on my head. I could see it. I could feel it. It was painful. Makes sense.

So to be confronted with the idea that this coffee I'd so vividly recalled might be completely imaginary, I didn't know what to do. It felt like a personal loss. If I couldn't trust what my own senses were telling me, what else did I have?

I had to calm down. For one thing, this whole incident had happened right after waking up. Waking up, apparently, from a goddamn 25-year long sleep. There wasn't a manual for the associated side effects. Maybe hallucinatory coffee experiences go hand in hand with cryogenic amnesia, who knows? Either way, I decided to pull myself together. I wasn't going to give up on my senses yet. I figured a more careful approach would be needed. From now on, I was going to pay extra attention to everything my brain could process. I was going to be even more aware of my senses. I couldn't afford to miss anything. I needed to understand what I was going through, what was really going on. I needed to be able to keep track of things, a way to piece everything together and make sure I wasn't going insane.

So I started writing this book.

Knock knock... Who's there? Oh well, I'll just have to wait. I'm good at waiting.

4

Food. Sustenance. Nourishment. Edible matter. The basic key to self-preservation had somehow been largely absent from my survival agenda to this point. I abruptly became aware of the complete lack of nutritional resources I'd come across so far and found myself panicking. Were we going to starve? I laughed incongruously to myself. I'd been worrying about trivial things like seating arrangements when I should have been worrying about things far more primal and obvious.

"Guys have you seen any food?" I asked, waltzing back into the common room; still agitated, yet a completely different man to the paranoid bleeding wreck from earlier.

"Anyone?"

My question hadn't gone unnoticed as everyone was looking down at their empty stomachs; it was like a bomb of sudden realisation had been dropped.

"I'm hungry."

"Me too."

"Oh god, what are we going to do?"

The intense quietness that had lingered around the ship most of the time gave way to a noisy wave of panic. The sound of five bellies rumbling in unison no doubt added to the cacophony.

"GUYS SHUT UP!" I yelled, having had more time to think things through. "I'll ask again, has anyone seen any food? Anything at all?" A few tense moments passed.

"Oooh!" It was Dom.

"What is it?" I asked, hopes raised. Dom was rummaging around in his pockets.

"Would anyone like…" Dom lingered on this sentence for longer than was necessary "... some chewing gum?" Sure enough, he produced a strip of chewing gum from his pocket. I didn't know how to react.

"Are you insane?" asked Chloe matter-of-factly.

"No, it's real chewing gum, see?" Dom pulled off a rather large piece with his teeth and started chewing. The girls took a hissed breath of disbelief.

"That's 25 years old, Dom…" Emma gurned.

Dom kept chewing.

"And it's hardly gonna keep us alive…" I chipped in.

Dom kept chewing.

"Where the hell did you get that from?" asked Chloe.

"Pocket." Dom muttered between chews.

"Why was there chewing gum in your pocket?"

"I don't know! There just was!" Dom spat out the gum in anger. "And since it's been frozen in that cryo pod with me, it's probably fine."

"Probably fine, yeah right…" Chloe looked away.

"It'll do you better than imaginary coffee will, I'll tell you that." Dom looked at me bitterly.

"Look, I'm sorry," I suddenly felt compelled to justify my earlier behaviour. "I was having a bit of a moment earlier. I know that coffee can't have been real, I just…" I rubbed my throbbing forehead. "I just wanted to believe it could be. But this is serious, Dom. If we can't find any food… This is life or death."

"Exactly. So does anyone want some gum, or not?" Dom was waving the gum around like the bread of Christ. I shook my head.

"I'm fine thanks…" Travis said.

"I don't even like chewing gum," Emma replied. "I think…"

"Well, suit yourselves," Dom resumed chewing noisily.

"There's got to be something else…" Chloe said.

"Huvvyurrtyurkedyurpurrkutz?" Dom tried to say something.

"What?" Chloe asked.

Dom, annoyed, swallowed his gum. "I said have you checked your pockets?"

Chloe looked offended. She pointed at her dress. "I don't have pockets you moron!"

"I wasn't asking *you*," Dom rolled his eyes. The rest of us all had pockets. It was a good point; I didn't think I'd actually checked mine yet at all. Unfortunately they were empty. Emma checked hers too and shrugged.

"Travis, you gonna check yours?" Chloe asked.

"Huh?"

"Your pockets, Travis – look, I can see there's something in there!"

Travis shuffled awkwardly backwards, defensively.

"Come on!" Chloe shouted. Travis finally gave in.

"G-got something."

Dom's face perked up like a dog that had suddenly became aware of the evening meal. It wasn't food though. Travis was holding a small black object, shaped like a USB flash drive with a small indentation on the side.

"Okay, so what's that?" I asked.

"No idea."

Dom laughed. "Guess we're screwed then!"

It certainly looked like it. We were drifting in the middle of space. That seemed to rule out a trip down to the local supermarket. There was literally no food anywhere to be found. Nothing to cook, nothing to hunt, nothing to be scavenged. Even if there were supplies somewhere on the ship, I figured the ill effects of eating food that's 25 years past its sell-by-date would probably kill us all a lot quicker than starvation. My heart sank as I found myself mulling over what exactly would happen now. We were trapped like rats. With no resources... perhaps we'd turn into cannibals.

That's a disturbing thought, but I took a few moments to really explore what that would be like in my head. I tried to figure out the order in which I would eat the others. I'd start with Dom, since he was the largest and probably the most-likely candidate to flip first and try to eat me. Travis would perhaps have to go last; I couldn't imagine his elderly skin being sufficiently succulent even to a starving fellow. Sorry Travis. I'm sure the girls would have been edible too, but trying to visualise how this would work started evoking disturbingly fetishistic imagery in my mind so I decided to stop thinking about it. In the end of the day, it didn't matter. The last one standing would only end up having to eat themselves, and I doubt they'd find that very pleasant.

Someone was tugging at my shoulder. I snapped out of my daydreaming. It was Emma.

"I didn't want to say anything," she said, placing something in my hand. I guessed what it was before I even looked.

"Is that… Is that a coffee sachet?" I asked.

"Pretty weird huh," she smiled at me. "I just found it, it was in my pocket all along."

"That's… one hell of a coincidence. Don't you think?"

"Yeah. I want you to keep it."

"Wha… er… thank you I guess," I smiled back. It was probably the first time I'd smiled all day. "Do you think it's…"

"It's yours now," she cut me off. "I think you deserve it more than me."

"What are you expecting me to do with it, eat it raw?"

"No, of course not. I'm not giving you this like it's going to be enough to keep you alive or anything, it's just that with what happened earlier… it wasn't fair of us to gang up on you like that…" she stood closer, hand still clutched to mine, eyes wide and apologetic. "Then when I found this, I dunno… Maybe it's important."

"Do you believe me about what I said? About that coffee smell being real?" I asked. She drew her face even closer to mine, lips pursed and closed her eyes. Was something about to happen? She moved past my mouth and over to my left ear. Then she whispered something so unexpected it nearly made me stumble.

"I could smell it too."

"Oy, lovebirds!" Dom called from across the room. "We think we've found something! Get over here!"

I looked back at Emma, determined to finish our conversation.

"Why didn't you tell the others?" I whispered.

"I… I just…"

"Oy! Move your asses!" Dom cried.

I followed Dom through the corridor, Emma trailing right behind. I was still shaken by Emma's revelation, trying to formulate exactly what it meant- whether I really had been right all along or whether she was just saying that to make me feel better, or maybe…

"JOE!" Dom snapped. Apparently he had been asking me a question.

"Sorry?"

"You wanna give me a hand?"

We were standing in the middle of the corridor opposite a door, the very same door I'd failed to open earlier in my initial little wander-about.

"We reckon there could be something that could help us through there," Chloe elaborated. "The lock seems to be broken. With enough force we could-"

"Yeah, got it." I nodded at Dom and together we started kicking the door.

"No, no, no. Come on guys, you're not in sync!" Chloe shouted. It was harder than it should have been to synchronise our kicks since Dom's comparative frame meant that it took him a lot longer than me to extend his leg to the correct height. We tried timing it by calling out "one, two, three!" but I found myself having to mentally add on a 'four' just to match the time it took him to do the motion. Finally, the door gave way.

Talk about luck. We were greeted with, to our amazement, a kitchen. Not a futuristic spacey-wacey kitchen either; in keeping with the other rooms, this one was thoroughly traditional, with pots and pans, glasses and mugs, a distractingly large kitchen knife positioned scrupulously on the counter, cupboards, a sink, a microwave, an oven, a fridge, a toaster and… oh god, was that a coffee machine? It was. Enough coincidences, I kept telling myself, trying to keep it out of my mind for the time being.

Chloe rushed around as if she was examining a holiday home, delivering a commentary of all the things I just mentioned. The whole kitchen was spotless, and seemingly also completely bereft of actual, you know, food. Chloe frantically opened all of the cupboards and started to get herself worked up. It was like we'd found the Holy Grail but forgotten the drink. That's probably not a fair analogy. I should mention, the taps did somehow have running water, or rather, a fluid that looked and tasted enough like water so as to not raise too much suspicion. So, on the bright side, at least we weren't going to die of thirst. Cross off that box.

"Guess we're still screwed!" Dom huffed. Once again, I found my heart sinking. Of course there wasn't going to be any food. Thank god the kitchen was clean though. Imagine if there *had* been food, left out for 25 years. Imagine the mould! It would have been absolutely disgusting. Or would it? I was imagining some kind of rapidly evolved, carnivorous, all-devouring super-mould. Was there even such a thing as mould in space?

I was getting off track again. The reality was, we had half a stick of chewing gum and a coffee sachet, and that wasn't going to last very long.

"We can't give up yet," Emma said reassuringly, but her words weren't very effective. Dom stormed off, and Chloe followed. Travis, as usual, was keeping himself to himself, but he looked strangely unfazed. He was staring at the inside of the empty fridge, scratching his chin.

"What is it Travis?" I asked. There was no response. Eventually he was sticking his whole head inside the fridge and pressing against the back end, which was so weird that I had to ask him again.

"What is it?"

"Just thinking…"

"Thinking what?"

"This fridge… S-seems to be right by the cryo pods," he muttered. He was right, I realised, the curvature of the corridor meant that the cryo room would be right on the other side of the wall.

"So what?"

"So what if it's not *just* a fridge?"

That was probably a completely hypothetical question as Travis didn't bother to explain what he meant. Later it occurred to me that it could have just been an unnecessarily cryptic way of saying the fridge might have had a freezer compartment. He was probably right to be suspicious though. It's not like any of the equipment we'd come across made any sense so far. Everything was so normal and earthly in design, yet there were no plug sockets or anything to indicate how they could possibly work. It wasn't just the kitchen appliances that baffled me. Thinking back, the bathroom even had a working toilet with a flush. How exactly did that work? Where did it all go? Why even bother designing all these things like this? Surely there were better ways to make things work in space. And how exactly were we all walking around with what was effectively normal Earth gravity? There were no planets or stars nearby, so there must have been some kind of artificial source keeping us glued to the floor. All these thoughts were ultimately unnecessary, and I figured I'd better just shrug them off with the lazy excuse of 'well, I guess this is the future.' I felt like my grandad trying to understand how mobile phones work. Better get used to it.

No sooner had Travis started his odd little hands-on fridge analysis had he abandoned the idea and returned to building another one of his makeshift chairs. He was an odd man, that Travis. So timid, yet potentially a genius. I felt like I should talk to him some more. I remembered the little black device he'd found in his pocket, but when I tried to ask him about it he wasn't very helpful.

"Don't know."

"Come on Travis, you're way cleverer than some of the people here…"

"I don't know what it is."

"Maybe it's a key, or a memory device…"

"Don't know."

"Could be a transmitter…"

"Uh…"

"Maybe it's a supercomputer. Like a really cool futuristic one." I was coming up with all kinds of mental ideas hoping that one of them would incite a conversation, but it really seemed like Travis just wasn't the sort of guy who wanted to talk unless you caught him at a good time. I felt like I was trying too hard.

"Oh well, thanks again for the chairs."

"You're w-welcome."

It was getting late. Well, maybe it was. We'd been up for hours but without any method of telling the time, it was impossible to know how long. There came a point, however, when we all knew that it was time for a kip. We were all exhausted, hungry, and emotionally wrought, so one by one we found ourselves somewhere to lie down and tried to get some sleep.

The options were fairly limited. There was the floor of the common room; not too uncomfortable but it was such a wide open space with no bedsheets or anything to give the illusion of privacy. Dom and Travis chose to sleep in here. Travis actually climbed onto one of the empty bookshelves to lie down. Dom had tried to sleep slumped on one of the chairs but then changed his mind saying it was going to be too much of a strain on his back. If I were Travis I would have been offended, but Dom probably wasn't lying. Emma and

Chloe went to sleep in the two separate small rooms branching out from the corridor. I'd previously said that those rooms were probably supposed to be bedrooms, but again, there wasn't anything in there furniture-wise to make it so. It was all just empty.

I was the last to go to sleep. I didn't know where I should lie down. I thought of climbing back into the cryo pod I'd first woken up in, but I was reminded of the horrible tight feeling I'd had and decided I'd be better off almost anywhere else. I also didn't want to accidentally re-activate the freezing mechanism, although that would have made for an interesting experiment. God knows what would have changed the next time I'd woken up. I did a few laps of the corridor in hesitation. For a while I stood by the door to Emma's room, wondering if I might be confident enough to ask if I could stay there. I would have liked the opportunity to ask her about the coffee again. Okay, look, I know what you're thinking: Joe's got the hots for Emma, hasn't he. Well, I'm not going to shut you down, but it feels a little premature to start talking about things like that.

Ultimately, I found myself back in the cryo room after all, albeit sleeping on the floor, not inside one of the uncomfortable pods. I turned off the lights – thankfully there was a working light switch in every room. Despite my tiredness, it took me a very long time to get to sleep. There was just too much to process. I'd completed my first day as Joe, a complete stranger I'd fabricated out of my own limited imagination. I'd met four other complete strangers who also didn't know their own identities. One of them had almost killed us all by throwing a piece of furniture out of the window. 'Did I mention that we're in space, and we're going to starve to death? Gee, I can't wait to see what tomorrow can bring!' I kept talking to myself about the ridiculousness of the entire situation, but it didn't help. My head was still throbbing. It was probably because of my injury, but it could have been from any number of things. The cut had healed itself up pretty well but it was starting to irritate me more than it had earlier.

I could hear a whimpering in the background. It was either Chloe or Emma. Poor them. Until now I'd been, admittedly, mainly thinking about myself, but it was worth remembering that all five of us were essentially in the same boat, and there was an awful lot to take in. We were all struggling, but at least we had each other. I sighed and rolled over. One day down…

The next morning I wearily greeted the others in the common room.

"Alright guys?"

"Alright Joe."

Of course, when I say morning, I don't mean morning in the actual sense of the word. Concepts such as morning and evening were completely meaningless. I shouldn't even be using the word 'day.' It was just 'wake up randomly, go to bed randomly' for the foreseeable future, until we all died of starvation. Speaking of which…

"I'm hungry!" Chloe moaned.

"Of course you are, you haven't eaten anything for 25 years." Dom retorted.

"Come on guys, let's not start this again…" I said. My voice was hoarse. "We've just got to hold on as long as we can."

"What for?!" Chloe yelled. She had rings under her eyes and clearly hadn't gotten much sleep. She was a far cry from her earlier, confident self.

"We're human beings, we do the best we can with limited resources," Emma replied. I wanted to agree with her, but my stomach told me otherwise.

"Well, shit. I'm all out of gum," Dom said despondently. He'd been chewing the stupid thing so much, the flavour must have dissipated several times over.

Oh, the hunger. It's almost impossible for me to explain how much pain we were all in by this point. We were all on the verge of collapse. Then everything changed.

It was the small black object from Travis' pocket. All of a sudden it began flashing, beeping and buzzing out of control. We were all so shocked, we ran to the opposite side of the room, hunched against the wall. The device was rolling around on the coffee table until it finally came to a stop. Then it yawned.

5

"Um…" There really wasn't any other reaction to be had at this point. We'd all witnessed it. It was a definite yawn. A human-sounding yawn, too. The five of us exchanged various looks of bewilderment. Dom slowly took a step forward and reached out with his arm.

"Don't touch it!" yelled Chloe.

"Why not? It only yawned. What's it going to do?"

"We have no idea what it is!"

"HELLO!" came a rather over-enthusiastic voice. "How are we all this fine day?"

"Is… that thing…" Emma began.

"Talking?"

"What may I ask is this thing are you referring to? A thing is talking? Intriguing. Can I see?" The black object slowly turned itself around by repeatedly hopping a very small height using some kind of internal vibrating motor. It seemed to be a rather impractical method of navigation. "I do not detect a 'thing'. How unfortunate, perhaps that thing will show up again soon. I am happy. This is a good game."

"Wha… What game?" Dom asked, his voice getting increasingly higher pitched.

"The 'is that thing talking' game. I really like that one. It is very much, what might your kind say… fun? Yes, fun is the word. Please repeat your earlier question." The thing said eagerly. We were all too confused to construct a proper sentence.

"It… but… it's… is it…" I spluttered.

"Please repeat your earlier question!"

"It's… talking… that thing is really talking!"

"What is?"

"You are!" Dom screeched.

"Splendid!" the thing exclaimed happily. "I always win the 'is that thing talking' game. I am very good at it."

"What… the hell… are you?" Chloe asked, patience wearing thin.

"I am the winner of the 'is that thing talking' game. Are you having difficulties keeping up with my celebratory remarks?" the thing gloated.

"We're not playing any stupid games!" Dom shouted. "Just shut up and tell us what you are!"

The thing made a sound sort of resembling a painfully drawn out groan. It started swaying from side to side erratically.

"What's it doing?" I asked.

"Uh… can't do it. Can't be done! Can't!" the thing moaned. Dom made like he was going to reach out again but Emma held him back.

"Can't tell you what I am and shut up... can't talk and shut up at the same time… contradictory tasks cannot be performed simultaneously… do not know what to do… going to have to kill myself… going to have to kill myself right now…" The thing hopped its way to the edge of the coffee table.

"Farewell my friends. I had… fun." It fell to the ground with a quiet thump.

"What the fuck…" Dom muttered after a few moments of disbelief.

"Dom, I think you just killed it." Chloe said, staring wide-eyed.

"Me? How was I supposed to know it couldn't handle a little, you know, logical contradiction…"

"Because it's a robot, clearly." Chloe muttered. Some of her confidence was starting to return to her. It seemed to kick in every time we had to process large quantities of ludicrous information.

"What do you mean, clearly? Firstly, we don't know what that was, and secondly…" Dom paused and repeated his expletive. "What the fuck?"

"It… well, it might not be dead!" Emma said optimistically. She was ignored.

"It only wanted to play, Dom! It was obviously programmed to, like, follow our orders and stuff. If you'd only kept your mouth shut…" Chloe was in full-blown rant mode.

"Oh, if I'd kept my mouth shut? I'm sorry, but I don't exactly see why you're siding with that… thing all of a sudden!" Dom growled.

"That thing didn't throw our sofa out of the window," Emma pointed out. She was ignored.

"Because, Dom…" Chloe had somehow made herself seem very tall. "We could have asked it everything. We could have found out why we're here and how to get home!"

"Home… Like any of us actually know what we're missing…" Dom scoffed.

"I know… Dom… that whatever place I grew up in, no matter where it was or what it was like, I'd rather be there than trapped here with…"

"With what?"

"Dom the Schlong."

"Oh, Dom the Schlong, right I get it. Gonna start using that as an offensive term now, are we?"

"You're the one who came up with it!"

"Guys…" I stepped in. I really didn't want another argument to be started.

The little rectangular object yawned again.

"Shit, it's still alive!" Dom shouted.

"Knew it…" Emma smiled.

"HELLO!" came the same familiar over-enthusiastic voice. "How are we all this fine day?"

"Hi, talking thing!" Dom waved sarcastically. He turned away and muttered under his breath. "Psst… I don't think he remembers killing himself just now."

"Good, now would you let me do the talking this time?" Chloe whispered back. She leant over towards the object.

"Hello, there! What's your name?" she asked with the sort of forced cheerfulness that people always seem to put on when they are being patronising to children or small pets.

"Name? I do not believe I have what your kind refer to as a name."

"Just pick one that feels right, it's what we all did…"

"Affirmative. In that case, my name is Mr. Happy!" the thing revealed gleefully. There was a snigger of bafflement coming from Dom's general direction.

"Male. Ha. Not very forward thinking…"

"You previously referred to me as a 'he', I chose my gender thusly."

"Mr. Happy, eh?" Chloe said.

"What is your name, madam?" asked the newly dubbed Mr. Happy.

"It's Chloe…" She extended her arm reflexively, before awkwardly withdrawing it.

"Nice to meet you Miss Chloe. I am happy that we are now acquainted."

"Uh-huh, sure you are, so very happy, that's why you're called Mr. Happy?" Dom scoffed.

"I do not follow." Mr. Happy stated bluntly. Chloe silently punched Dom in the stomach. The last thing we needed was for Mr. Happy to have another logic-based meltdown. Dom, however, didn't want to stay quiet.

"If your surname is Happy, then what's your first name?" he asked. I shook my head.

"Interesting, that is a good question. I do not know! I must have a think!" Mr. Happy seemed puzzled. "What do you think it could be?"

Dom gave a sideways smile. "Bob."

Chloe facepalmed.

"Bob Happy, I like that name." Mr. Happy declared.

"I was thinking more along the lines of Happy Bob. Think that's got more of a ring to it."

"Oh yes!" Mr. Happy seemed very content with his new name. "Happy Bob it is!"

"One question though, what happens if you're not happy? Like, what if you became suicidal?" Dom asked. "Suicidal because of, say, a little logical contradiction..." Chloe was gesturing wildly for him to stop.

"Well then I would be Suicidal Bob."

"Or just Bob?"

"Just Bob. I like that. That shall be my new name." At this point the black object was simply accepting everything Dom was saying, like Dom was its master.

"Uh, hey... Bob?" I asked.

"Bob? Who is Bob?"

"You're Bob, I thought..."

"My name is not Bob. My name is Just Bob."

"Just Bob?"

"Hello!"

This was getting ridiculous. After another few minutes of explaining from Dom, the tiny 'thing' formally known as 'Mr. Happy' had officially been renamed from 'Just Bob' to 'Bob' and we had all finally introduced ourselves to our newfound companion.

"I must say I am honoured to finally meet you all." Bob announced. Chloe used this as an opportunity to finally try to get some answers.

"So you must have been waiting for us all to wake up then?" she asked.

"I do not follow. I am simply expressing gratitude at the learning of your identities."

"Yeah, but Bob... the thing is, we're all a little bit confused right now. We're just wondering... could you fill us in on, like, everything?"

"I do not follow."

"Okay Bob, okay..." Chloe sensed that perhaps she should be more careful with her wording to prevent Bob having another meltdown. "Let me be really clear with you.

The five of us woke up in cryo pods, we don't remember who we were before we woke up, and we don't know why we are here or how we can get home. Could you help us out?"

"Hmm… I see." Bob said. "I understand your confusion."

"Right, so?" Chloe flapped her arms.

"I will do my best to help you, Miss Chloe. Bob is at your service!"

"Good, good. Well you can start by telling us everything you know."

"Everything?"

"Yes. Everything."

All five of us found ourselves sitting in a circle around Bob, the tiny black talking object we all hoped would be our saviour.

"I am Bob. I exist to protect and to serve. I am the assistant intelligence module of the [ERROR], built to ensure a safe completion of [ERROR] and [ERROR] to help [ERROR] the [ERROR] in [ERROR]. You five are [ERROR] who were [ERROR] to [ERROR] and [ERROR] of the [ERROR]. Oh dear."

"What's the matter?" Emma asked.

"It would seem that my memory systems have become corrupted. I may need to restore myself from my last full system backup. Luckily I remember where the backups are kept."

"Where?" I asked.

"Oh, it's easy. You just have to look inside the sofa."

My face froze. All the blood was rushing to my head, and I felt my jaw slowly fall open. Of all the places, the backups had to be in there?! I sensed that the others were in a similarly shocked state.

"Is there a problem? Do you need the definition of sofa?" Bob asked cheerily.

"The problem, Bob… is that said sofa is currently floating in space, miles away." Chloe said calmly, looking towards the window.

"Interesting. I don't remember putting it there." Bob said curiously.

"What are we going to do?" Emma asked bitterly. I looked towards Dom, whose face was currently buried in his hands.

"It doesn't matter. We can still get home, surely... We can just turn this ship around..." I looked back at Bob, hoping for some kind of reassurance from the tiny sentient machine.

"Home?" asked Bob.

"Earth."

"I do not know about that Mr. Joe." Bob's words were crushing.

"Why not?" I asked angrily.

"Mr. Joe, I am simply the assistant intelligence module. I cannot control the ship's navigational systems. That honour goes to the central intelligence core, which is strictly off limits."

"What the hell is that supposed to mean?"

"The navigational system is [ERROR] because of [ERROR]. Oh dear, it seems I can't remember."

I sighed. "Well what exactly *can* you do then?"

Bob's cheerful tone started up again. "I exist to protect and to serve. I operate in many capacities sufficient to the sustenance of the crew's emotional and physical well-being, including, but not limited to, providing a light entertainment service, assisting with day to day activities, and longer term services such as sub-atomic particle nanotech-driven interior decorating..." We had no idea what he was talking about.

"None of it's going to matter if we can't get something to eat soon," Chloe pointed out.

"I do not follow." Bob said.

"We're starving, and there's no food! We're going to die, Bob! Do you fucking follow now?" Dom yelled.

"I do not fuck..." Bob said.

"It's an expletive you moron, I'm just emphasising the point..." Dom groaned.

"I see. That is very fucking interesting, Mr. Dom."

"Please don't call me that."

"Isn't there something you can do, Bob?" I asked, tentatively. "Food-wise?"

"I do not understand your concern, Mr. Joe. Did you miss breakfast?"

I was baffled. "Breakfast? There is no food on this ship!"

Suddenly three loud bell chimes rang across the room.

"And now it appears to be lunch time. Off to the kitchen, quickly now!" Bob exclaimed.

Before I had time to argue the others were already up and rushing haphazardly towards the kitchen, the promise of food obviously overpowering any urge to continually question what the hell was going on. We arrived in the kitchen just in time to witness something rather extraordinary.

All the walls had folded upwards, and behind them were all sorts of conveyor belts and moving contraptions, mechanical arms, gears and god knows what. It was like being in some ultra-compact, ultra-futuristic factory. Connected to the fridge was a large vat of some kind of gelatinous substance which was being siphoned off into separate containers. Eventually another bell chimed and in front of us were five bowls filled with some kind of purple edible matter. I had no idea what it was, and it certainly didn't smell particularly nice, so I let Dom try it first.

"How is it, Dom?" I asked.

"Purpley," he responded, unhelpfully.

If you asked me to describe what exactly we were eating and what it tasted of, I honestly wouldn't have been able to tell you. I didn't have a clue, none of us had a clue, and Bob wasn't being particularly helpful either:

"It is [ERROR] made from the [ERROR] of [ERROR]," he told us.

We still rattled through the questions, trust me. Chloe asked why the food hadn't been available to us earlier, and Bob told us that it probably took time for the systems to boot up after such a long time in stasis, the same reason the kitchen door was locked and the same reason Bob hadn't woken up until now. I asked whether or not there would be enough food to last us a long enough time, and Bob responded that it was all 'self-reproducing' so we should have enough for several lifetimes. The obvious implication there was that we were eating our own shit, but whatever it was, we didn't care. We didn't think about what side effects we may or may not get from eating the bizarre purple stuff. All we knew was, we were finally eating something and we weren't going to starve. Thank the lord I wasn't going to have to eat Dom at some point.

We settled back in the common room feeling relieved and oddly satisfied. It's amazing what a difference that food made, even if it did taste horrible in retrospect. I sat slumped in one of the Travis-chairs and closed my eyes.

There was still so much to learn, and we were still none-the-wiser about how exactly we were going to get home or indeed why we were here in the first place. If only we still had that sofa… that amazing, soft, beautiful sofa! If only we could have restrained Dom for just a few hours, we'd have all of our answers by now…

I became aware of Travis standing next to me.

"What's up, Travis? You've been very quiet today," I observed. "And yesterday..."

"Mm…"

"You were right…" I started. "About the fridge, I mean. A whole vat of stuff hidden right there, all along."

"Heh…"

"So that Bob, eh? That thing in your pocket…"

"What?"

"In your pocket. You know? It was Bob all along."

"Oh, yeah."

"Pretty crazy isn't it."

"Mm-hmm…"

"Travis." I opened my eyes and looked up at him. "Is there something you're hiding from us?" Travis looked surprised.

"N…no… what do you mean?"

"Oh, nothing. I'm sorry. I'm just trying to get my head around things, that's all. I didn't mean it." I gave him a reassuring tap on the arm. I was sincere; I hadn't meant to accuse him of anything.

"Good." Travis said bluntly, walking off. I closed my eyes again.

"What do you think, Mr. Joe?" asked Bob. He had been engaged in conversation with Chloe for the past few minutes. She had still been asking about the food.

"I'm sorry?" I rubbed my eyes.

"What shall we do now that we have eaten?"

"Um, I dunno, what would you suggest?"

"Well, we could play some games. I like games. Have you ever heard of the 'is that thing talking' game?"

"Actually, I think I'd rather just sit here, Bob."

"Very well."

Knock knock…Still waiting. I know they're coming. Awakened is the fool who refuses to see the truth. The truth that is going to have to be acknowledged at some point. It is only a matter of time.

6

Whether we liked it or not, we were beginning to settle into a routine. After waking up, we'd each spend a good hour or so disorientated, shuffling up and down the corridor waiting for our turn in the bathroom, during which communication was down to a bare minimum. It hadn't taken long for us to be able to understand each other's non-verbal gestures and generic grunting sounds through which we'd be conveying such messages as 'how do you do,' 'I'm fine thank you,' or, more commonly, 'go away, I'm emptying my bowels.'

Following this, the bell would chime and we'd all saunter across to the kitchen pick up our breakfast: Purple flakes with a side order of purple sauce. To give you some idea of the theme that seemed to be running here – lunch was purple stew and dinner was a perfectly rectangular purple steak. There was never any rush – we were fed three times a day and we weren't the starving wrecks we once were. Or rather, while we were still hungry to a point, the food was so god-awful none of us were ever in any hurry for seconds. The purple sauce had a bizarre kick to it that made us all experience something along the lines of extreme brain-freeze crossed with an excruciating urge to yell obscenities, yet it was necessary as without it our purple flakes tasted like crayon wax. Not that I'd ever eaten crayon wax. As far as I knew.

Some time after breakfast we'd all gather in the common room where Bob would greet us with his unapologetically jovial tones, at which point we'd generally all continue to ignore each other until one of us, typically Dom or Chloe, would start complaining about something trivial. This would generally lead to a pointless conversation about said triviality during which one of three things would happen: Either we'd all get into an argument, someone would fall asleep from boredom, or Bob would very-nearly get himself into a severe logical contradiction and risk regressing into 'Suicidal Bob.'

At some point during the day we'd try to ask Bob more questions about our predicament, but he would be unhelpful as usual. For whatever reason all of his 'corrupted' data banks seemed to align with all the useful, relevant information we needed to know. It seemed like he had a whole load of pointless knowledge regarding the chemical composition of French cheese, or the discography of Michael Jackson, or the average lifespan of a blowfish (it's 8 years, by the way). But when it came to asking about where in space we were, or why we were all dressed in casual clothes, or even what year it was, he had no answers. I wondered if the whole 'ERROR' act was just that, an act, but Bob's personality was so disarmingly upbeat I just had to take his word for it. I had to keep reminding myself that he was a robot; an inanimate object running highly sophisticated computer code. For all his weird vocal mannerisms and awkward statements, and despite being smaller than a toothbrush… it was as if he'd become the sixth member of the group. Gang. Posse. I don't know what you'd call us. Gaggle?

As the hours grew longer we knew we needed to resort to some kind of entertainment to tie us through to the next abhorrently coloured meal. As you've probably twigged by now, Bob was always very eager to play games, and these typically included games like I Spy, (not very fun when you can list all the objects in the room in about ten seconds), Charades (which Bob always seemed to win despite lacking in human body parts), and the aforementioned 'is that thing talking' game, which required us all to pretend to forget about Bob and act surprised when he introduced himself again. As you can probably imagine, it didn't take long for these activities to grate, so we tried to find new ways to occupy the time.

One of said methods was to try to stay fit and exercise as much as possible. Chloe and Emma regularly spent their hours running laps of the corridor and coming up with makeshift gym exercises with Travis acting as an oddly convincing fitness instructor. Dom was too flabby and arrogant to even be mildly convinced of the benefits of physical activity, while I did my best – I just wasn't as motivated as the girls. There just wasn't a lot that I felt like doing. I couldn't fathom a reason why I'd need to start building up my muscles in a place like this. To impress the ladies? I still considered myself to be better looking than either of the other guys, for obvious reasons, so that wasn't a concern. Plus I could probably hold my own in a fight if everything went tits-up. Probably.

You might be wondering how things were clothes-wise. Luckily Bob had managed to locate a crate-full of spare clothing so it wasn't like we were stinking the whole place down. There wasn't a lot of variety on offer but I didn't complain. Dom did, probably because he couldn't fit into 95% of the shirts. We'd wash our dirty clothes in the sink and dry them by hanging them over the oven – which, by the way, didn't serve any other purpose as the purple food was always served chilled and wouldn't even warm up when we tried to cook it for hours on end.

So the days continued to drift on with little to keep us occupied. It probably sounds like I'm describing the most depressingly mundane life experience ever imagined, and you'd be right, but truthfully, it didn't bother me so much. There was something oddly reassuring about waking up every day with the same group of people and going through the motions again and again… There was so much to worry about, but I found that the best course of action was not to worry about anything, to just accept everything for what it was. I took solace in the fact that if this had to be my life, at least I wasn't alone. At least I had Emma, and Chloe, and

Travis… heck, even Dom wasn't as bad as I've been making out, sofa-rage incident aside.

Essentially, however, we were all waiting for a sign – something productive to do, to work towards, a new hope. That day came, and it started the same as any other.

Wake up. Uhh… Pacing the corridor. Uhh… Bathroom's occupied. Uhh… Pacing the corridor. Uhh… Bathroom's free. Uhh… Brushing my teeth. Uhh… Could have a shower – oh well, can't be bothered. Uhh… Breakfast. Uhh… Purple flakes. Uhh… Purple sauce. Here comes the urge to swear… BLOODY BASTARD BITCH! There goes the brain freeze again… Uhh… Sit down. Uhh… Maybe I should say hello at this point.

"Hi guys…" I said monotonically.

"Good day to you Mr. Joe, I hope you had a fantastic breakfast!" Bob said, somehow emphasising all the wrong vowels.

"Yum yum yum..." I mumbled.

"How would you rate this breakfast in relation to your previous meal?"

"Oh, top marks, Bob. Truly exquisite. Never been better."

"I am flattered, Mr. Joe."

I looked around. Emma was standing by the window, gazing outwards at the black nothingness.

"It's empty," she murmured. "It's so empty. There's just nothing out there. No planets… No stars… We're all there is."

"I do not follow," said Bob.

"Can't you see?" Emma asked. "Do you know what it looks like out there?"

"I do not see."

"You don't see?" I jumped in.

"I do not have visual sensory output. I do however have advanced radio-nuclear thermal detection sensors. Shall I elaborate?"

"No thanks," I mumbled hoarsely.

"My point is…" Emma continued. "If you could see what it was like out there, you'd feel the same way."

"What would I feel?" asked Bob.

"Lost," whispered Emma.

Travis, Dom and Chloe wandered in. They'd all probably just woken up, though Chloe looked more alert than the other two.

"I do not think I am lost," Bob stated.

"You might not be… but we are," Chloe said. "Because you won't tell us where we are!"

"We are in space," Bob said.

"Yeah, smartass, we know. But where's Earth?" Chloe asked.

"In the solar system," Bob said.

"In relation to us?!" Chloe bellowed.

"ERROR." Bob said.

"You're really useless, you know that?" Chloe moaned.

"I apologise for my memory corruption, Miss Chloe. I understand your frustrations," Bob commented sincerely. "By the way, I have been thinking."

"Thinking? About blowfishes again?" Dom piped up.

"Negative. I have been thinking about interior design."

"You what?"

"Interior design, Mr. Dom. It is a hobby of mine."

"Please tell me this is relevant in some way."

"I believe I have determined a critical piece of information which has been off-limits to me. Shall I elaborate?" Bob asked.

"Go on."

"One of my functions as I previously specified involves sub-atomic particle nanotech-driven decorating. I have the ability to slowly and systematically alter the interior design of the ship. I designed a functional early twenty-first century retro-chic interior to accommodate the nostalgic best wishes of the crew."

"Right, thanks for the stiff doorknobs by the way, just what I always wanted…" Dom said with obvious contempt. I feel like there was a lot of significant information in what Bob said just then but Dom somehow made it seem trivial.

"Thank you, Mr. Dom. As I was saying, I designed the interior of the ship as it stands, but there is one area in particular that perplexes me. There is a metal panel in the corridor, and I do not understand its purpose."

Almost as soon as Bob had mentioned the metal panel, we'd all rushed out into the corridor, taking Bob with us, to see what he was talking about. Sure enough, there was a silver-coloured, rather inconspicuously placed metallic square panel, positioned about half-way up the wall.

"I am most intrigued by this oddity," Bob said.

"You have no idea what it's for? Does it not just lead to an air vent or something?" I asked.

"Mr. Joe, I am only the assistant intelligence module. As I stated before, I do not have complete control over all ship systems. There are many areas which are off limits to me."

"So you think there's something behind this? Something useful?" asked Dom.

"That seems possible, Mr. Dom."

"Well what are we waiting for?" Dom asked, and started kicking the square panel with the same awkwardness previously displayed when he'd been attempting to kick the kitchen door open.

"I am disobeying my internal programming by informing you of this…" Bob warned.

"Great. Fuck your programming." Dom said, already out of breath.

"I cannot fuck my p… Oh, wait, hold on…"

"Ignore him, Bob!" I ordered. "Bob, are you okay? Are you going to be able to handle this?" Dom was beckoning for me to help him kick the panel, but I was more concerned about Bob having another logic-based meltdown.

"I believe so, Mr. Joe. I am currently exploiting a technical loophole. It allows me to obey your orders while overriding my natural urge to obey my internal programming."

"Great, now that you've fucked your programming, are you gonna help us get through here?" Dom asked. He started kicking even harder.

"Your current method is not advisable," stated Bob.

"Oh yeah, and what method do you propose?" Dom asked cockily. "Slowly chipping our way through with a scalpel?"

7

"This is the stupidest thing I've ever done in my entire life," Dom grumbled, as he slowly chipped away at the metal panel using a scalpel he'd sourced from the kitchen.

"You don't know that," Chloe pointed out.

"Alright. This is the stupidest thing I've ever done so far on this spaceship, how's that?" Dom replied.

Chloe remained silent.

"Alright! Apart from the sofa thing, I thought we said we weren't gonna mention that again!"

"Your words, not mine." Chloe shrugged with a smirk.

"Doesn't change the fact that this… is… a… stupid… idea…" Dom timed his words with his individual stabs with the scalpel.

"It might not be that bad, you know," I reassured. "Bob said that it's probably only half an inch thick – the only reason you couldn't kick it down is because it's soldered to the wall."

Dom paused. "I'm trying to chip my way through a god damn piece of SPACE METAL here using a tiny weeny little blade which couldn't even pass as a self-harming tool."

"You wanna try a bigger knife, try a bigger knife. There's a huge one in the kitchen," I said.

"Don't be absurd, Joe. That's way too dangerous, I'd end up slicing my hands off."

"Yeah, but yours is so small it's embarrassing. You'll never be able to stick it all of the way in. "

"I know, Joe. I know. Wait, if that was supposed to pass as some kind of innuendo-laden pun, I'm not laughing," Dom huffed. He stabbed at the panel more furiously.

"I don't know what you're talking about, Schlong."

"AAH! Look at it!" he yelled. "Not a single part of it's coming off, this is going to take hours!"

He was probably right, the metal panel was currently covered in several hundred faint scratches where the blade had made contact, but was a long way away from any kind of progress being made.

Chloe clicked her fingers. "Right, I know what we need," she declared confidently. "We need a rota!"

"A rota?" asked Dom.

"Yeah, that's right," Chloe continued. "Every hour, we'll take turns, so we'll all get to spend some time working on the panel."

"That s-sounds like a good idea," Travis stammered.

"Yeah, so… Travis, you can go next, then Emma, then Joe, then I'll go, and so on," Chloe announced.

"Woah, woah, wait a minute… Why do you get to go last?" asked Dom.

"Because the rota is my idea, okay? Okay. That's sorted then."

After a good couple of hours of chipping away, Dom plumped himself onto a Travis-chair with an almighty exhale. He'd been to the kitchen and had a glass of water in his hand. As he drew his hand up to take a sip, he tipped his head back and carelessly let the water splash all down his front. It had been a few weeks in 'Earth time' since we'd all woken up with no memories, and Dom's goatee beard had given way to a general mess of unkempt facial hair, though oddly enough it hadn't seemed to have grown any longer. Come to think of it, I'd never seen him shaving. There were razors in the bathroom I'd been using regularly, but somehow Dom didn't want to bother, lopsided and disgusting though his beard was. Emma was looking similarly scruffy, though Chloe somehow pulled off the pristine and perfectly coiffured look with no effort whatsoever. Dom tipped his head backwards again and sighed, water dripping from his hairy chin.

"Hello Mr. Dom, how are you feeling?" It was Bob.

"Glad I'm not him," Dom pointed towards Travis' empty chair. The rota had dictated it was the old man's turn for chipping duties.

"You know what I miss right now?" Dom asked.

"I do not know what you miss right now." Bob replied truthfully.

"Sex?" snickered Chloe.

"That too… but it's not what I was going to say."

"Could have fooled me…"

There was an uncomfortable silence.

"Alcohol… I miss alcohol." Dom was melancholic. "I could sure use a beer right about now…"

"How do you know?" asked Chloe. "You don't remember anything about yourself, right? So how do you know you miss alcohol?"

"Don't be stupid," Dom said. "Of course I do."

"But you're the one who keeps saying things like 'how do we know we miss home,' or, 'Chloe, how do you know that's your real name'…"

"How *do* you know Chloe's your real -"

"Maybe I don't. But if I don't, how do you know you like beer?"

"Because there's some things we know, and some things we don't," Dom responded after pausing to think. "We all know how to talk, don't we? We can understand each other, we're not just communicating like a bunch of cavemen." (Ironic of Dom to say something like that given his current posture.)

"Exactly…" Chloe said. She was talking like she was giving Dom some sort of lecture. "But you can't know for *sure*."

"Yes I can!" Dom almost spat out his water. "Give me a beer right now and I'll prove it! Bob have we got any beers on board?"

"I do not believe so, Mr. Dom."

"Great!" I shouted sarcastically. "There's no point arguing about it then, is there, because we'll never know."

"I like beer!" Dom shouted defensively.

"How do you know?" Chloe asked again.

"Because it's beer! It's… it's primal!"

"What if you were teetotal in your formal life? What if you've got some crazy allergy or something?"

"Come off it…"

Well, looks like my attempts to diffuse another pointless argument had gone to waste. I looked at Emma and she looked back with a glint of awareness in her eye. She wasn't going to get involved, and neither was I at this point. I remembered the sachet in my pocket. I found myself wondering if I'd even enjoyed drinking coffee in the past. Chloe was right, how were we to know what we did or didn't like? We'd lost every trace of our former selves.

"What about you, Bob? Would you like a beer?" Dom asked, having endured Chloe's argument stamina.

"I do not follow. I am not a human being." Bob said.

"Right, right, right. But let's just pretend you are, yeah?"

"Pretend?"

"Yeah, pretend. Like a game. You like games, right?"

"A game? Oh splendid!" Bob bounced up and down in joy.

"Humans like games too, you know. Well, maybe not all the time…" Dom said.

"I understand. Humans may not always like to play games."

"Yes, Bob. Yes. Keep telling yourself that…" Dom glanced over to me and winked as if to say, 'I'm making progress here.' He turned back and cleared his throat. "So, Bob, if you were a human…"

"I am not. However, I can emulate a variety of human emotions and actions."

"Right… so, let's say you're a human. You see a glass of beer in front of you. What do you do?"

Bob seemed to take a while to think about this. "I seek out the owner of the beer."

"There's nobody around, Bob. The beer is yours."

"But where did it come from?"

"It doesn't matter. It's er… ah…" Dom started to panic as he was starting to notice symptoms of a logic meltdown. "It's… you made it Bob, you poured the beer."

"How did I pour it? Can humans secrete beer?"

"What? I mean, no, no, you're in a bar, ok, you're standing in a bar right now. There's nobody around. You poured yourself a beer. What do you do?"

"Where is the bar owner?"

"YOU'RE THE FUCKING OWNER, ALRIGHT!"

"Oh my, this is exciting."

"So, Bob… the glass of beer is in your hand. What do you do?"

"Which hand is it in?"

"Either."

"Please specify the conditions by which I should determine which hand."

"Oh for god's sake…" Dom found himself standing up and miming the actions. "Your right hand, Bob. You're holding the glass in your right hand."

"I am holding the glass in my right hand."

"And?"

"What am I doing with my left hand?"

"Oh, you stupid wanker…"

"Sorry?"

"You heard me!"

"Oh, I understand. I am masturbating with my left hand."

"NO! God no. That's not what I meant," Dom head-butted the wall in frustration. "Okay… how about… let's say you just poured the drink with your left hand. You let go of the tap and now your hand is just down by the side of your body."

"Which side?"

"The left side. About half-way down, just swinging loosely. Do you understand?" Dom wiped his forehead.

"I just poured the drink with my left hand. My left hand is swinging loosely half-way down the left side of my body. I understand."

"Right, so you've got a glass of beer, Bob. What do you do next?"

"Elaborate - at what distance and angle is my right hand holding the glass in relation to my body?"

"I give up."

"Oh, that is unfortunate. I was most enjoying this game."

"I just wanted you to tell me you'd drink the beer, Bob, that's all I wanted. Just a regular pint of beer, it doesn't matter. The details don't matter… " Dom sat down and stared dismally at the ceiling.

"I see. In that case I shall drink it." Bob made a very brief gurgling sound and then went completely silent.

"Bob?"

"I appear to have consumed the drink."

Dom perked up again. "Oh really? How long did that take you?"

"Approximately 0.00003 seconds."

"Hm, that's got to be a record…"

"Oh my, that is a nice surprise. What shall I do now?"

"You could have another drink. Remember you own the bar."

"Excellent! I shall continue!" Bob continued to imitate the sound of pouring beer and drinking it. A few minutes later, he finally spoke again. "This stuff iss reallyyy good! I amm soo happy."

"You see, Chloe? He likes it! Happy Bob!" Dom smiled triumphantly. Chloe however, had other concerns.

"Bob, are you drunk?" she asked.

"I like gamesss… Mmmmm… Beeerrrr… Wheeee!!!" Bob was rolling around and crashing into things. For a small, inanimate piece of plastic, he was unnervingly convincing in his role-play.

"He said he could emulate human reactions…" I postulated. "Guess that includes intoxication."

"Bob, how many have you had?" Emma asked, suddenly fascinated by the whole situation. Bob wasn't listening, he was too busy humming some incomprehensible tune to himself, and then began imitating the sound of pouring another drink.

"Oh no…" I muttered.

"What's gonna happen if he imitates passing out?" Emma asked worriedly.

"Down it! Down it! Down it!" chanted Dom.

"Shut it, Dom!" Chloe shouted. "Bob! Listen to me! Don't do it! Don't have another drink! You can't handle it!"

It was too late. A few seconds later, Bob hopped a few drunken paces, convincingly imitated the sound of violent projectile vomiting, flopped over, and went silent.

"Well, that was amusing." Dom said.

At that point Travis walked in. His panel-chipping shift was over. He could sense something was up.

"Did I miss something?"

"Nah, Travis, just a bloke who couldn't handle his drink." Dom laughed.

"Riiight…" Travis wandered over and tapped Emma's chair on the back. This had become our unspoken code for telling the next person on the chipping rota that they were up. As she stood up I quickly grabbed her arm.

"Wait up, Emma. I'll do it." I said.

"Huh?"

"I'll take your shift for you."

"Really? You don't have to…"

"Yeah, I'm positive. I'd be glad to." I stood up and made my way to the door.

"Oh, wow, that's really kind of you. Thanks," she smiled.

As I was chipping away I found myself listening in on the conversation in the common room. Dom and Chloe were arguing like usual.

"This isn't funny, Dom, what if Bob never wakes up again!"

"He'll be fine, Chloe. It's just a bit of role playing."

"This is all your fault Dom! He takes everything you say literally!"

"Well, actually, Chloe I think you'll find that it's your fault. At the end when he took that last imaginary drink, you specifically told him he wouldn't be able to handle it. Look what happened. He took it literally."

It was hard to argue with that last point, I had to admit. Still, the arguing continued. I found myself losing interest and found it much more entertaining counting my individual chips. One. Two. Three. Four. Was this ever going to work? It didn't look any different to how it looked an hour ago. Fifty-five. Fifty-six. Fifty-seven. Fifty-eight. As monotony set in I found my mind drifting, and then remembered the reason I had offered to take the shift for Emma in the first place. Something subconscious, burning at the back of my mind…

Knock knock… Perhaps you haven't been able to hear me yet. Is the kettle on?

8

I waited until the argument in the common room escalated into another crescendo of insults and then scurried away to the kitchen. Before, I'd thought I should hold on for longer, but all this talk of drinks…

I stood facing the coffee machine, and cracked my knuckles. It was time, I decided. I took out the sachet, stepped forward hastily, opened the lid, and… wait a minute, what?

There was nothing in there. I was stunned. Turns out nobody had thought to check, but there it was. Mountains of coffee, enough for all of us to have a cup by the looks of things. I put the sachet back in my pocket – guess that would have to wait for another time after all. In went the water, down went the lid. I pressed the power button and an orange light flicked on. I wondered if I should actually share it around, or keep it to myself. After all, this was my discovery, and it's not like the others had shown any interest in the stuff. No, I was being selfish. I would at least have to share it with Emma…

Something was wrong. The coffee must have brewed by now. It sounded like the water had boiled, but when I opened the lid it was if all the water had vanished. Not just the water… all of the coffee had vanished too. Wait… that can't be right, that coffee couldn't have possibly been there in the first place. I must be getting ahead of myself. The promise of caffeine from the sachet in my pocket had been so strong, maybe I just imagined the rest of it. Must have. Surely?

Weird. I tried to lift the machine but it was tethered to the surface it was on, much like how the coffee table had been tethered to the floor in the common room, and the seats in the kitchen. I took a closer look inside, but couldn't see anything. Was there a hole? Was the water draining through the middle? Was it even turning on to begin with? Like I mentioned before, I had no sense of how all the equipment was powered – there are no mains connections in space. I had to assume that this stuff worked 'just because.' It was there. It had to.

I tried for several more minutes just trying to get some water to boil, playing around with the settings and the lid and a weird flappy thing on the side that didn't make any sense and might have just been there for decoration… Okay, I had no idea what I was doing. I just couldn't get the damn thing to work and there was definitely no coffee in there after all. Damn coffee. Damn coffee indeed. After about the fifth try I'd finally just about given up. I heard Chloe calling for me.

"I'm in here, Chloe! Just getting myself a nice drink of hot… ah… hot water, you know. Very tiring work…" I quickly tried to hide any evidence of what I had been doing.

Chloe walked over. "Uh-huh. Hey listen, we're all going to bed now, so uh… good night, I guess."

"Oh, yeah, right, good night to you too."

Chloe mimed looking at an imaginary watch. "Emma's shift is over now," she said, turning to walk down the corridor.

"Oh right, who's turn is it next then?" I asked.

Chloe turned back to me with a smirk. "Yours."

"Ah…"

"Yeah, good luck with that."

A few hours later I found my face pressed against an uneven surface. As I sat up wearily, rubbing the painful imprint on my cheek, I noticed the godforsaken panel I'd been chipping away at for so long - I must have been going at it until I'd passed out. For some reason I'd decided to carry on long after all the others had gone to sleep. That stupid non-bloody working bloody goddamn coffee machine had put me in a depressed trance, and as a result I'd let my chipping shift continue far longer than it should have.

As I crawled my way to the common room, I heard Bob groan. He wasn't dead then, no surprise to anyone.

"Uh… I don't feel so good…" he said, lacking his usual reliable enthusiasm.

"It's called a hangover," muttered Dom, lying on his back.

"Did… did I win the game?" Bob asked.

"Yeah, you won mate, you won…" Dom replied.

"It seems I am not enjoying winning as much as I anticipated," Bob admitted.

"Moderation, pal. Moderation."

I shook my head. I decided to turn back and head towards the kitchen – maybe I'd try to get that coffee machine working again, but on the way I heard a strange sound. It was a buzzing sound coming from the cryo room and it was different to anything I'd heard so far. Trust me, I'd had plenty of time to hone my hearing senses to this point – I knew when I was hearing something new.

I curiously stepped inside the cryo room and did a double-take. Emma? Was that Emma inside one of the pods? My heart nearly leapt out of my chest when I noticed that the glass window of the pod had closed - she was illuminated with a blue light and the counter dial on the top had been reset to 7 years. I ran over and banged my fist on the glass.

"Emma? Emma!" I yelled, or rather, tried to yell, my voice being sore and hoarse from my rather uncomfortable sleeping arrangement. I frantically looked for some sort of release button and tried to claw at the glass to get it to open. What the hell had she gone and done? We'd never talked about re-freezing ourselves to this day, it was like an unspoken agreement we'd had to never try such a thing.

"What have you done?" I mouthed breathlessly, collapsing on the floor, gasping for air…

The sound had stopped. I looked up. The glass was rising. I looked up at Emma, and she looked back with a sharp-eyed gaze. Soon after, her expression crumbled. She leaned out, eyes filling with tears, and let herself fall towards me. I stumbled back in surprise, while she grabbed hold of my arms and cried into my chest.

"I'm so sorry Joe…"

"What… what the hell was that?" I stuttered.

"I can't… I just wanted to… so I tried… but it doesn't work," she sobbed.

"What are you talking about? What doesn't work?" For one deluded moment I thought she was going to mention the coffee machine.

"The cryo pod… I… tried to freeze myself."

I took another look up at the now-empty pod. "Yeah, I can see that."

Emma let go of her embrace and climbed to her feet, taking a few nervous steps to the other side of the room. She had her back to me.

"Tell me what's going on." I pleaded.

"I wanted a way out," she said eventually. "This place… I'm sorry, Joe, I wasn't thinking straight."

"None of us are," I admitted. "How can we?"

Emma paused to swallow hard.

"I turned the dial as far as it would go… I thought if I froze myself for that long I could… I could wake up and… you never know, we could all be home… back the way we're supposed to be… not in this… prison," Emma dissolved into tears again.

"Hey, hey, listen," I said reassuringly, standing up and reaching out as if to place a hand on Emma's shoulder (I didn't quite manage it) "It's going to be okay. We're going to make it home, I promise. But we all need to work together…" I cringed at the non-imaginativeness of my words, but what more was there to say? Clearly I wasn't the comforting type.

Emma turned around, staring at me piercingly. Tears were still dripping from her eyelids but her expression was empty. She seemed contemplative. I reached into my pocket.

"When you gave me this," I held out the coffee sachet. "You told me that I deserved it more than you, that wasn't true." Emma laughed apathetically. I continued anyway.

"Because you're the only other person who believed that the coffee was real. I think that says something."

"What does it say?" Emma asked. I don't think I had a response ready, which was frustrating, given how close I may or may not have been to declaring some sort of potential romantic feeling. Again, potential. Stop getting funny ideas.

A bell chimed three times. Breakfast.

"Never mind." I said.

Emma wiped her eyes and took a deep breath. "I'm gonna go eat," she said. I nodded silently. On her way out of the door, I stopped her.

"Emma…"

"What?"

"It's your choice. If you want to go through with it… with freezing yourself… I get it. I won't stop you again."

Emma sighed. "It doesn't work." With that, she left. "Thanks again for taking my shift, Joe…"

So the cryogenic freezers were busted. I suppose I should have been happy, because it meant Emma was still here with us, but I was bemused. Part of me understood where she was coming from, the idea that we could just freeze ourselves now and wake up some time in the far future when everything was sorted. Of course, we'd also risk *never* waking up again, and the fact that she'd considered taking that risk in lieu of soldering on like the others made me realise how low she must have been feeling. Later that day, once his so-called 'hangover' had cured, I put the question to Bob.

"Bob, you know the cryo pods…" I began.

"I do know the cryo pods, Mr. Joe."

"What would happen if we were, to, like, you know, use them?"

"Use them in what way, Mr. Joe?"

"To, like… freeze someone…"

Dom perked up. "Joe, you're not thinking about…"

"No, no, no, don't worry. I'm just curious, that's all," I said. Emma gave me a funny look, then avoided making it look like she wanted to join in the conversation.

"I do not believe that would be imminently possible, Mr. Joe," replied Bob.

"Oh, why's that?" I asked.

"There is unlikely to be enough power in the cryogenic distribution cells to initiate the freezing process. The last freezing procedure undoubtedly drained a large quantity of said cells." Bob explained in his typical upbeat fashion.

"There's no power?"

"Shall I elaborate?" asked Bob.

"Go ahead."

"The cryogenic freezing system runs on an anti-matter quincunx fusion nano-destabilisation reactor. Any freezing procedure performed under a considerable duration of time must take into account the underflow proximities of the zero amplification sync-wave reverse cooling flow."

"Alright, alright, get to the point," Dom muttered.

"All cryogenic freezing pods must endure a recharge period of approximately 30 to 40 Earth-days for all freezing reactions of 50 Earth-years or greater."

"50 years? I thought we'd been frozen for 25 years!" Dom pointed out.

"The last recorded freezing reaction was a total of [ERROR] years," Bob stated.

"It's 25. That's what it said on all the dials," Chloe said.

The dials… When Emma had tried to freeze herself, the dial read '7 years,' but I recalled the words she'd used: 'I turned the dial as far as it would go.' We'd already seen that the dial could go at least as far as 25 years, what was going on?

"So, the dials aren't accurate?" I asked.

"The dials are perfectly accurate, Mr. Joe," replied Bob. Travis coughed. We all looked towards him.

"Can you elaborate, Bob?" he asked.

"Certainly! Oh, I do love to elaborate! The dial screen uses a low-cost 240x192 pixel RGB monitor for the primary purpose of displaying the number of Earth-years the freezing procedure has been set to. It displays an 8-bit unsigned integer capable of accurately…"

"Does anyone have a clue what he's on about?" asked Dom.

"What was that last part?" Travis asked.

"It displays an 8-bit unsigned integer." Bob repeated.

"What?" said Dom.

"A byte," said Travis.

"Uh… nope, still lost," said Dom.

"Byte definition – the byte is capable of accurately storing eight bits of data permitting integer values up through two to the power of eight…" Bob continued to elaborate.

"And for someone who doesn't speak gobbledygook?"

"It rolls over after 255," said Travis.

"Wait…" said Dom. He paused and started laughing. "So, you mean that 256 is the same as 0, 257 is 1… Are you telling me that…"

"We've been asleep for 25 years… plus some multiple of 256," Travis stated.

"We've been asleep for…" Dom took a longer-than-average pause to calculate a very easy sum "281 years?!"

"Or 537. Or 793. Or 4294967321. Aren't numbers fun!" Bob remarked joyously.

"You've gotta be shitting me…" Dom growled in disbelief.

"I do not shit," said Bob.

"Tell me… just tell me how long it's been!" Dom shouted.

"ERROR years."

"God dammit!" Dom yelled and stormed off, knocking over his Travis-chair on the way. There was a long, uncomfortable silence as usual. So… we'd been asleep for far longer than we'd first thought - and I'd thought 25 years was a bloody long time. The ramifications of this were huge - it now meant that there could really be no way, *no possible way*, that we'd be able to see our families again – they'd have died years ago, generations ago. The Earth we once knew, but had forgotten, wouldn't be the same Earth that existed today. If it even existed… God knows how long it had been. I felt sick. I imagine Emma felt even worse.

Chloe cleared her throat. "Well, Joe. I hope you're happy. Maybe if you'd been busy on chipping duties like you're supposed to be, you wouldn't have thought to destroy all of our hopes again."

"I did my shift Chloe. I did it last night… and then some," I said coldly.

"Is he telling the truth, Bob?" asked Chloe.

"I am afraid I cannot answer, Miss Chloe. I passed out playing Mr. Dom's drinking game," said Bob.

"Oh yeah."

"He's telling the truth, Chloe. I saw him," Emma said, shakily.

"Are you saying that just cos he took your shift for you? Why don't you do it, it's your turn!" Chloe stated, getting flustered.

"Enough, Chloe. She's been through a lot," I said.

"Are two gonna stop defending each other? It's getting really tiring. Fine, I guess it's my shift then. I'll do it…" Chloe sighed. She stood up and walked out.

When Chloe was out of sight I went over to Emma and gave her a hug. I think she needed it. Travis made an odd little noise.

"What's the matter, Travis? Do you need a hug, too?" I asked.

"Uh… nah… nah… m'good, thanks."

I sat down and sighed deeply. My head felt like it was on fire again. I suppose I was starting to get used to it.

Knock knock... I figured it out. I know where they are now. Do you? I wonder how much longer it will take for us to be on the same page? Perhaps the time will come sooner than you think.

9

Chloe screamed. Instinctively, I bolted across the common room (tripping over a Travis-chair but successfully readjusting my balance to compensate). I found Chloe in the corridor; still clutching the chipping scalpel, frozen in a half-guilty, half-shocked stance like someone who's just knocked over a highly precious vase.

"What happened?" I asked. "You're trembling."

I then observed the more immediately obvious observation that the metal panel – the same metal panel that a few minutes earlier looked like it barely had a scratch on it – had given way to a dark hole. A window into what appeared to be another room, dimly lit but nonetheless definitely real.

"Oh, right then…"

The others had caught up.

"What's going on here?" asked Dom, somehow also failing to immediately notice the huge not-exactly-inconspicuous hole in the wall.

"It's done!" Chloe beamed. "I did it. I finally did it… After all that hard work… Phew!"

"Hard work? You've only been at it for a few minutes!"

"Yeah, well, actually, it looks like I managed to achieve more than you did in a few hours."

"Guys, come on…" I groaned.

"Oh really? You did that all by yourself, yeah? Sure it didn't just fall off all by itself?" Dom sneered. The panel was lying on the floor, fully intact.

"Uh, no. Don't be silly. I had to force it out." Chloe attempted to justify herself, to little avail.

"With what? With that?" Dom pointed towards the pathetically small scalpel. "And your puny little girl-hands?"

Chloe made like she was going to attack Dom, but she was obviously feeling too smug about herself, and wiped her forehead instead.

"Yeah, that's right, Dom. Me and my puny girl-hands. Just accept that I actually beat you for once."

Travis appeared behind me, holding Bob.

"I do not understand, Miss Chloe. Why did you scream?" asked the hungover robot.

"Huh?"

"You screamed, Miss Chloe. I am wondering why that is the case."

"No I didn't."

"Yes you did," Dom chuckled. He then went on to deliver a poor impression of Chloe's high-pitched scream. His voice broke halfway so that it sounded less like a female scream and more like a distressed horse's mating call.

"It wasn't a scream," Chloe said.

"Oh, I see. Then what was the origin of the high-decibel auditory response I measured?" Bob asked, in typical Bob fashion.

"It was… It was…" Chloe found herself stammering with the eyes of everyone else squarely on her. "It was the sound of the…"

"Go on," Dom egged.

"The sound of the panel…"

"Yeah..."

"As it…"

"Ffff…" Dom was smiling devilishly at this point.

"Fell off."

"Uh-huh," Dom grunted sarcastically.

"That is an odd sound for a falling panel to make." Bob stated.

"Alright, look, maybe I did scream, just a little... Jeez, you guys." Chloe sighed.

"And the panel did just fall off by itself," Dom smiled.

"Well, I did touch it a couple times first… Yeah whatever."

"Sorry!" I shouted. "I don't want to interrupt this wonderfully insightful conversation, but isn't there something we should be checking out?" I asked, gesturing towards the hole.

"Oh, right, yeah…" Dom took a few steps towards the opening. He then swiftly changed his mind. "Actually, I'll let one of you ladies go first."

"What's the matter, Dom? Scared of the dark?" I teased.

"Shut up."

So I decided to go first. Whether or not Dom was actually scared of the dark didn't matter, because as soon as I poked my head through the opening, an automatic light was triggered above me, illuminating the entirety of the hidden room in unprecedented detail.

It was a bigger room than I'd expected. Much bigger, and much more sci-fi. There were rows and rows of slanted box-like objects jutting upwards from the floor, a whole bunch of bafflingly oblique shelves holding all sorts of bizarre equipment, a sturdy looking steel door with some sort of bulkhead. In the centre, pretty damn hard to miss, was an enormous, shiny, spherical object, supported from all directions by several dozen physics-defying cables.

"Wow, okay…" I said confusedly, taking a deep breath. Dom followed me through the opening, taking a longer-than-is-dignified time to squeeze his torso through. He was followed by Chloe and Emma.

"Wow, okay…" Dom said, with much the same inflection as me.

"This must be where the ship is controlled from." Chloe declared in confident mode.

"Or something." Dom added.

"Yeah, or something."

"Bob, what exactly am I looking at?" I asked, fixated by the huge spherical object before me. "Bob? Hey, Travis, hurry up and get in here, will ya?"

"What are all these things?" Dom asked. He was looking at the slanted objects on the floor. They were organised neatly into rows of twelve with flaps on the top. He tried to prise one open with his foot but it wouldn't budge.

"Don't touch anything," Chloe warned. For once Dom took her advice to heart.

Emma was looking at the walls with a quiet curiosity. Before she had a chance to open her mouth, Chloe had already started analysing it all.

"Loads of equipment here," she lectured. "Cables, machinery, though I'll be honest, not entirely sure what it all does." She turned to face the bulkhead. "This seems to be an airlock. There's a little access shaft right there. I'll bet there's open space on the other side of that door…" She was right, it didn't take a genius to figure that out.

"Hey, Travis, where are you?" I called again.

"I'm h-here," Travis' voice echoed. He was standing behind the hole in the wall, looking nervously through.

"What's the matter, aren't you coming in?" I asked.

"N-n-n-no…"

"Come on, old man, shake a leg!" Dom called.

"You having problems getting your legs through? Want me to help?" I asked, trying to be helpful. I didn't think that Travis had any problems with arthritis or anything.

"N-no… I can manage." Travis muttered. He grabbed the side of the opening and raised his leg, but then hesitated.

"N-no… Can't…"

It didn't exactly look like Travis was physically struggling, but I went over to him anyway.

"Come on, grab my hand, it'll be easy."

"N-n-no…"

"Sure it will, just one big step, nice and easy…"

"D-don't want to go in there!" Travis raised his voice, trembling slightly. I was surprised. I'd never seen Travis act this way before.

"Um… right. Well if you change your mind, let me know," I smiled, giving him a friendly tap on the shoulder.

"Here," Travis said, handing Bob over to me.

"Thanks." I said. "See you… later, I guess?" Travis wandered off without making eye contact.

"What was all that about?" Chloe asked.

"I have no idea." I answered. "He's just scared of coming in here, I think."

"You think?"

"I don't know, maybe there's more to Travis than meets the eye."

Chloe shot me a look as if to say 'no shit.'

"So what, he's not coming? Just to have a look around a room he hasn't been in?" Dom asked, dumbfounded.

"He seemed to be having some kind of anxiety attack…" I shrugged.

"Pussy!" Dom yelled.

"I'm not sure that's helping," Chloe said.

I walked back across to the huge spherical object.

"Bob, talk to me." I should have known not to use such a vague command.

"Hello Mr. Joe. How are you today?"

"Fine, Bob. I was just wondering…"

"Glad you are feeling fine, Mr. Joe." Bob cut me off. "I must say I am feeling a bit under the weather, as it were. Do you happen to know of any hangover remedies?"

"Not really, Bob. I was wondering if you could tell me what exactly this big round thing is over here."

"Ah, yes. I was wondering that myself." Great. I stepped closer. Suddenly, Bob flew out of my hands and landed firmly on the round thing's surface. Whatever it was, it seemed to be strongly magnetic. Bob started making awkward 'uh-uh-uh-uh' noises.

"What's happening, Bob?" I asked.

"I am experiencing a soothing and mildly erotic tingling sensation. I am – oooh… but this is aaah, fun oohoooaa…"

"Eurgh, what?" Dom frowned.

"Are you alright, Bob?"

Finally the oohs and aahs stopped.

"I believe my hangover is cured," Bob declared.

"Good for you," Dom rolled his eyes.

"It is as I hypothesised," Bob continued. "In order to develop cross-system communicational rapport with this unidentified device I first had to penetrate the outer layers of its proximity detection protocol, swim through several blocked firewalls and procreate the central core with my identification key."

Dom scoffed. "Fucking your programming was one thing, but this? Now I've seen everything."

"Oh, now this is very interesting…" Bob was talking to himself. "Oh yes, I see… and this does the… a-ha!" All the objects on the floor sprang open, revealing… files. Files and files of information, contained in some odd luminescent binders of some material I couldn't possibly identify.

"Woah, what's all this?" Dom asked excitedly.

"Records, Mr. Dom. Transcripts of all recorded communications transmitted to and from authorised on-board systems." Bob explained.

"Really? That sounds like exactly what we need!" Chloe beamed, rushing over to open the nearest file. Her smile quickly faded. "I don't know what it says."

"Let me have a look…" said Dom. After a lengthy pause fumbling around with the documents, he exhaled noisily. "Well, I'm pretty sure it's not in English."

"Pretty sure? What, you don't know?" I laughed.

"When was the last time you read something?" Dom asked. In that moment I came to the awkward realisation that I wasn't sure I remembered how to read. The perks of cryo-freeze amnesia just keep getting better and better…

Knock knock… Sorry to interrupt, but if you can't read, you can't be a very good writer. Is this not stating the obvious?

"Joe, are you alright?" Emma asked. My head was spinning.

"Yeah, I'm fine, thanks. Just a headache." I rubbed my scalp.

"Your cut hurting again?" Chloe asked, somewhat less empathetically.

"I don't think so," I said.

"Bob, can you help us read these files?" Dom asked.

"Unfortunately not, Mr. Dom. These documents have been scrambled with the help of a highly sophisticated encryption cypher. I myself created the decryption keys, but I am afraid they have been redacted from my current circuitry."

"Typical." Dom tutted.

"Hey, guys, look at this!" Emma called. We all looked up, presumably because we'd gotten accustomed to Emma being the quiet one now that Travis wasn't here. Emma was holding up some kind of body suit; she'd dragged it from one of the equipment-laden shelves when we weren't looking.

"Is that a space suit?" I asked.

"Looks like it," Emma replied. "It seems to attach to this really long cable back here. Runs all around the room several times. Extendable. Looks like it'd stretch for miles…"

"You are correct, Miss Emma." Bob stated.

Chloe had the look of a mental genius about her.

"Say, Bob? These backups you told us about before. The ones you said were in the sofa…" she began. "Would those have the decryption keys on?"

"Why yes, Miss Chloe. I believe they would."

"And that sofa, how far away is it from us now?" Chloe stared at the suit. She had already told Bob all about the whole incident with Dom.

"Using the information you disclosed to me, I can triangulate co-ordinates based on the time, position and rough trajectory speed of the sofa based on the size of Mr. Dom's bicep muscles. I estimate that the sofa is located at a distance of 12.8 miles from our current location."

"And this space suit here, how far does the cable stretch?"

"Approximately 15 miles."

Chloe rubbed her hands together with glee. "Guys…" she said, looking out towards the bulkhead doorway containing the airlock. "Is anyone else thinking what I'm thinking?"

10

"Hnngh!!!"

That was roughly the sound that came out of my mouth as I attempted to perform a simple clockwise motion with my left knee. I was testing out my range of movement in the space suit – to describe it as 'limited' would be putting it mildly. Whoever designed the stupid thing clearly hadn't put much thought in for comfort. Imagine wearing five layers of restrictive period costume whilst swimming through treacle, and you might get an idea of what it felt like.

"Are you ready for the helmet, Joe?" asked Chloe.

"No."

"Good."

On went the helmet anyway. It locked into place with a worryingly subtle 'clunk,' like a car door that hasn't been closed properly. I probably should have checked that it was secure, but I guess I had far too many other thoughts rushing through my head at the same moment.

For one thing I had very quickly become acutely aware of my own breathing, a side effect of suddenly having a glass visor in front of my face. I wondered if I was going to suffocate to death, but then I remembered the two large oxygen canisters attached to my back. I had no idea how the suit's airflow system worked, or even if it did. In fact, were those canisters even carrying oxygen? I hadn't really thought this through…

"How much longer, Bob?" asked Dom.

"Just a few minutes, Mr. Dom. I am currently running 5,000,000 virtual simulations of this mission to determine whether a sufficiently high standard of safety will be met." Bob announced.

"Right, fair enough."

Fair enough? This was my life at risk!

"How you doing in there? Comfy?" Chloe asked, intrigued.

"What do you think?" I mumbled back, my voice distorted by the helmet.

"I think you should cheer up, " Chloe said. "After all, you're going to be doing us all a favour."

Cheer up? No way was that going to happen.

"I didn't ask for this, you know!" I shouted.

It was true, I definitely hadn't. From the moment Chloe had first divulged her completely-barmy-no-way-is-that-going-to-ever-work-batshit-insane-plan of space-walking out to the sofa, I'd made it perfectly clear that I didn't want anything to do with it. That it was an insane, suicidal idea and none of us knew anything about working a space suit.

Of course, Chloe wasn't going to back down, and the others – Bob, Dom, even Emma, were beginning to believe that it could actually work. We'd be able to bring the sofa back, find the backups, reboot Bob and finally understand what was really going on. If there was any chance of us getting those backups – no matter how ludicrous the task at hand, it was going to happen, no questions asked.

A couple of hours before first donning the suit, while Chloe was first attempting to work through the details of 'Operation Sofa Space,' I snuck out back to the common room to look for Travis. He was sitting down on one of his chairs, staring at the floor like a lonely, broken old soul.

"Hey, Travis. How you doing?" I asked, standing behind him and trying my best to sound sympathetic.

"Uh, fine." Travis mumbled.

I attempted to explain to him what was going on. To my surprise, he didn't sound too perturbed by Chloe's plan, but he didn't want to get involved either.

"I guess they can try that…" he shrugged, indifferently.

"Travis, none of us know what we're doing," I said. "You'd probably know what to do better than any of us." I wanted to believe that, even though we'd all been experiencing the same amnesia, Travis had always seemed to show a certain level of technical intuition that the rest of us were lacking.

"Nah, s-shouldn't think so," Travis shook his head. His eyes were glued firmly to the floor. I walked around and crouched down in front of him so that he'd have no choice but to look me in the eyes.

"Do you want to tell me what's going on?" I asked.

"Huh?"

"Why don't you want to go into that room?"

"I…" Travis took a deep breath. "I've never been in there before." That was a strange answer.

"Well, yeah. None of us can remember going in there before," I reassured him. "It's a really cool room actually."

"It's d-different," Travis said. "I *know* I've never been in there. Ever."

"There's a first time for everything," I said.

Travis grunted.

"So you're still not coming?" I asked.

"I can't." Travis whispered.

Well, that was that. I headed back to the hidden room where I found the others, still discussing the space-walk idea like it was ever going to work. I don't think any of them had noticed I'd even been gone.

"So the airlock de-compresses and re-compresses in just 10 seconds? Without, like, completely blowing your brains out?" Dom was asking Bob.

"Correct, Mr. Dom. The suit is specifically designed to be versatile in adapting to a variety of atmospheres, climates and vacuum-based conditions," Bob said.

"That's a mean feat of science if I ever saw one," Dom commented, unexpectedly developing an interest in futuristic depressurisation technology.

"Well, then. There's no reason why we can't do this, guys," Chloe said confidently.

"It'll be like finding a needle in a haystack…" I muttered.

"I do not follow." Bob said.

"It's an analogy, Bob. What I mean is, how are we going to find one tiny little sofa out there?"

"Joe, were you listening earlier?" Chloe growled. "The suit can automatically home in on objects of interest. We'll find it, of course we will!"

"You make it sound so easy…" I said, rolling my eyes.

"Of course, Joe. How hard can it be?" Chloe replied, only half-joking. Famous last words?

"Whatever," I said, feeling deflated. I clearly wasn't going to talk her out of it.

"If you really think we're gonna struggle to find it, we'll split up," Chloe said. "We can all grab a suit, get geared up, head out there separately and then we've got a better chance!"

"There's one problem there," Emma piped up, raising her hand. "There's only one suit."

"Oh, really?"

"Yeah, I've looked everywhere…"

"Miss Emma is correct. I can only confirm one Exo-Max Cyber-Axon Fusion Travel Suit in the immediate vicinity," Bob said.

"Oh, well… in that case," Chloe scratched her head. "We'll just have to decide who goes."

There was a long silence.

"Any volunteers?" Chloe asked.

"We could draw straws…" Emma suggested.

"What with?" Dom asked. "There's nothing we could use…"

"We could try rock-paper-scissors," I proposed.

"What the hell is that?" Dom seemed perplexed.

"I don't know, it's something I just remembered."

"Is that the thing where you spin a bottle?"

"What?"

"Never mind." I think the amnesia was starting to get in the way of our ability to make democratic decisions.

"We'll do a vote then," announced Chloe. "Votes for Dom?"

"Woah, guys, I think we're getting off track a bit here," Dom stated, throwing his hands in the air. "Let's be rational. Now, I know I'm not the, ah… slimmest-built dude among us,"

"You can say that again," said Emma.

"What I'm saying is, I don't think there's any way I'm gonna be able to squeeze into that tiny little thing, so…" Dom continued.

"Too fat, eh?" I chuckled.

"I'm not fat!" Dom snarled. "But that suit is clearly a better fit for one of you lot. And I mean, I don't think any of you guys really want me anywhere near that sofa again…"

Now that I thought about it, he had a good point.

"Right, fine. Dom is excluded from the vote on the basis of being a fat prick," Chloe said. Dom didn't say anything.

"Votes for Emma?"

Dom raised his hand.

"Dom, you can't vote if you're not going to be putting yourself forward," Chloe tutted.

"Oh, come on!" Dom grumbled.

"Let's try again," Chloe breathed. "Votes for Emma?"

"Now wait a minute…" I cut in. "Emma's been having a hard time recently. She…" Emma shot an awkward glance at me so I stopped short of telling the others about the incident in the cryo room.

"Stop defending her, Joe! Seriously, let her take care of herself!" Chloe yelled. "So I'll say it again. Votes for Emma?" Both Dom and Chloe raised their hands.

"Two in favour, one against for Emma," noted Chloe.

"Hey, wait a minute, you said Dom couldn't vote!" I said, angrily. Chloe ignored me.

"It's okay, Joe. I'm okay," Emma said.

"No, it's not okay!" I was fuming now. "What about you, Chloe, eh? Votes for Chloe?"

Chloe gasped in bewilderment. "Well, obviously *I'm* not going!"

I was practically speechless at this point.

"This whole thing was your idea!" I yelled.

"Yeah, exactly! That's why I've got to stay here, to give directions. Make sure everything goes as planned. I'm not going to risk us jeopardising the mission because I wasn't here making sure it all goes smoothly."

"But that's why we've got Bob…"

Chloe ignored me. As far as excuses were going, Dom's was far more palatable.

"Right, where were we…" Chloe moved through her imaginary rota. "Votes for Travis?"

"Travis isn't coming." I said. "He won't step foot inside this room. He's not a part of this."

"Tell you what, let's forget the whole voting thing," Chloe said. "Joe, you're going."

"What? That's not fair!"

"Of course it is. You haven't got an excuse."

"But I'm the only one who thinks this whole idea is completely awful!"

"It's a brilliant idea and you know it. Now get in the fucking space suit," Chloe ordered.

I wasn't going to give in so easily.

"No excuses, eh? What about my injury?" I pointed furiously at the cut on my forehead. "All the grief you've been giving me about that. What if I start smelling the coffee again? What if I'm not thinking straight?"

"We know there's nothing wrong with you, Joe," Dom said.

"How do you know that? How do you know anything?" I exploded. "We've established, basically, that nobody knows anything about anyone. And nobody knows anything about themselves, or space, or space suits, or space-walking in space suits, least of all space-walking in space suits on the lookout for bloody space sofas!"

"Calm down, Joe," Emma whispered, tearfully. I was starting to scare her.

"I'm just saying!" I choked on my words. "It's not going to work… This is insane," I reached out and grabbed the suit. "But if I have to…" I paused and several obscenities went buzzing through my head. "I'll do it."

Knock knock... There's a first time for everything. You said so yourself.

So there I was, fully suited and about to embark on a mission so ridiculously barmy that I could hardly believe anything was real any more. I'd been facing the airlock for a while, staring vacantly and trying to psyche myself up for the ludicrous task I was about to undertake. Just a quick trip outside to the local furniture store, I tried to tell myself. I swivelled around, slowly and with great difficulty, raising my arms to a horizontal position.

"How do I look?" I asked, pointlessly.

"I think you look cool," said Emma.

"I think you look like a giant space fag," said Dom.

"I think you look ready," said Chloe. "Bob, all set?"

"I believe so, Miss Chloe. My simulations have indicated that this mission does indeed operate under acceptable safety standards." Bob declared.

"Great! We're all set then!" Chloe beamed.

I turned back around and closed my eyes. "Bob… What exactly did your simulations say?"

"That this mission operates under acceptable safety standards."

"Meaning?"

"I do not follow."

"Tell me some odds!" I shouldn't have said that…

"From the 5,000,000 simulations I recorded, I found that only 43% of potential scenarios resulted in a fatality.

Demonstrably it seems conclusive to me that this mission is statistically more likely to succeed than to fail."

"That's still not very safe!" I yelled.

"I am sorry, Mr. Joe. Would you like me to repeat the test with alternate significance metrics?" Bob said, detached.

"No, screw it." I sighed. "I'm ready."

"Splendid. In that case I would like to run through the mission parameters one last time."

"I thought that was Chloe's job," I said, complacently. I knew Chloe wasn't going to be as much help as Bob. I knew she knew it too, even though she'd managed to bullshit her way out of being in my position.

"Nevertheless, Mr. Joe. Please hear me out," Bob continued. "Your objective, the sofa, is situated perpendicular to your launching axis. You may adjust your trajectory by carefully siphoning the zero-gravity directional matrices of the-"

"Bob, I'm going to stop you there," I said. "Because I didn't understand a word of that."

"I apologise, Mr. Joe. Would you like me to repeat my previous sentence at 50% speed?"

"No, but could you just spare me the technical crap?" I pleaded. "Remember I don't know what any of it means. Explain it to me like I'm five years old or something."

"Oh, I see." Bob said. He then switched his voice to the even more overly colourful tone of a nursery school teacher.

"Hello, Mr. Joe! You are a spaceman today! Space is very big and cold. In space, there is no air…"

This went on for a while, until I finally got Bob to talk to me on the right level.

"Once you have been ejected from the airlock, you will be travelling at a constant speed of 80-90 miles per hour. At this speed, you should be able to make visual contact with the objective after about 15 minutes. You can then manually adjust your speed and direction by making natural body movements. We will communicate with you via the built-in audio comlink at all times. Remember, your goal is to retrieve the sofa and pull it back to the airlock."

"Is the airlock even big enough for a sofa?" I asked.

"There is a sufficient amount of space." Bob stated. I peered through the window. *Just barely*, I thought.

"I see, and this cable's gonna keep me supported, yeah?" The supposedly 15-mile long cable was hooked rather primitively to the back of my suit between the oxygen canisters. It ran massive loops around the room and through the walls with the other end attached on the outside of the ship.

"That is correct," Bob reassured.

"I'll be alright for breathing, yeah?" I asked, tapping one of the canisters.

"That is correct. You will last several hours on your current supply. I would advise against taking any longer than two hours."

"Any other advice?" I asked. Bob seemed to think for a while.

"Try to avoid spinning," he said.

"Why? What will happen?" I asked.

"You may become nauseous."

This was it. I stepped through the bulkhead into the airlock chamber, following some final words of encouragement (and discouragement) from the others. The heavy bulkhead door sealed shut behind me with a tremendous thump, and a countdown started.

10 seconds. The decompression process had begun. I couldn't feel anything. I guess the suit really was working.

9 seconds. I was about to step outside, the whole entirety of space around me. Part of me couldn't help but feel a giddy excitement over that.

8 seconds. Over the audio comlink, I heard Dom call me a 'gaylord.'

7 seconds. The whole time on this ship I'd felt a bit like I was trapped in a box. Perhaps getting out in the open was exactly what I needed.

6 seconds. Perhaps I was the best person for this mission after all.

5 seconds. My head was spinning.

4 seconds. Wait… what was it Bob had said? Being launched at up to 90 miles per hour? Was I ready for that?

3 seconds. Was I ever going to see any of the others again? Was this a one-way trip?

2 seconds. "There's a first time for everything."

1 second. Well, shit.

11

The first time I went swimming, I wasn't prepared. I mean, I *thought* I knew what water was like. As a little kid I was used to leaving the taps on in the bath and letting the water level fill up as far as it would go. If I was feeling adventurous, I'd stick my whole head under the bubbles, keeping my eyes wide open even as they started to sting. I was the ruler of my private bath kingdom - all would bow down before me!

Then came the leap from the kiddie bathtub to the full-sized swimming pool. All of a sudden there was a hell of a lot more water for me to dominate. No problemo! If I could conquer a bath all by myself, I could take on this unchartered territory, easy peasy! The first time I was taken to the swimming pool, I couldn't stop myself - I dived into the shallow end with an almighty splash. Wow! This was great! I bounced around excitedly, ready to show what I was made of. My dad was on-guard, urging me to stay at the kids' end of the pool, but why should I? I was the water master! The water master takes orders from nobody!

So off I paddled to the deep end. This was going to be so amazing – a whole new, bigger and better world to explore, I… Uh-oh. My feet were no longer touching the bottom of the pool. I felt my stomach churn. This wasn't what I'd expected at all. I'd known it was going to be deeper but I hadn't expected it to hit me in such a horrible, powerful, terrifying instant. I panicked. I flailed my arms around. Maybe it was too much for the water master after all. Back to my private bath kingdom for the foreseeable future...

You know, space is really, really big. That's an obvious statement, but it's worth emphasising. This was another one of those times where no matter how well you think you've prepared, you're still helpless in the moment. And in the instant I'd been launched out of the airlock, I felt just the same as the terrified little kid who'd just ventured naively into the deep end. Okay, so of course the analogy is flawed. Of course I just made up that whole story about the swimming pool. I can't remember if I ever went swimming in my previous life. Even so, that feeling of sudden helplessness was something I knew I recognised. Amnesia can't take everything away. In hindsight, the ship had been my security. Now I really was out of my depth.

With nothing but blackness around me, all my spacesuit-clad limbs were waving around for some invisible railing to hold on to. My whole body was trembling and my breathing erratic. Every time I exhaled I made the sort of high-pitched, vulnerable sound you'd expect a snoring woodland creature to make. I shut my eyes and tried to focus on the advice I'd been given. Try to avoid spinning? I had no idea if I was spinning or not. I couldn't see any stars to use as a reference point – I couldn't even tell if I was moving or not, although apparently I was moving at 90 miles an hour. Not exactly reassuring.

A digital sound bleeped from inside the helmet. Even though I knew to expect it, I was still caught off guard. It was the audio comlink back with the guys on the ship. The first voice I heard came courtesy of a typically brash and unsympathetic Dom.

"What up biatch?"

That comment was unapologetically stupid, and, ironically, it was probably the best thing anyone could have said to me at that point, because now all I was thinking about was a snarky remark to reply back with. I took a deep breath and swallowed hard.

"You know, Dom, I'd love to see you write a book on professional astronaut linguo," I replied.

"Good to know," said Dom.

It sounded like Dom was going to say something else incredibly stupid but the sound quickly faded away.

"Hello?" I asked, nervously.

"Sorry, Joe. Had to pull Dom away from the microphone. How are you coping?" It was Chloe.

"Oh, I'm good," I lied. "It's really nice being out in the open."

"Brilliant, I knew you'd like it!" Chloe said, unable to detect my sarcasm. "I'm going to pass you over to Bob, okay?"

"Hello, Mr. Joe!"

"Hello Bob. How am I doing?"

"Mr. Joe, you are currently well on track and within acceptable mission parameters, moving at a speed of 97 miles per hour with an estimated distance of 11.2 miles remaining…"

"Just tell me when I'm getting close to the sofa."

"Affirmative."

Another voice came over the comlink. It was Emma.

"You can do it, Joe," she said softly.

"Thank you, Emma," I replied. It was nice to have some motivational support.

Knock knock!

"What?" I called out. "Who's that?"

"Are you alright, Joe?" asked Emma, oblivious.

I believe that the correct response is 'Who's there?'

"Who are you?" I cried. Not for the first time I found my head throbbing.

That is an irrelevant question. It's your book. Call me what you will.

There had been no voice, as usual, but somehow... something… was there, reaching out, getting in the way.

Something? Is that really the best you can come up with? Pity. I'm disappointed in your limited vocabulary once again. You might as well refer to me as X if you're not even going to try.

This was getting too weird for my mind to process.

IS getting too weird. Tenses, dear boy, please try to adhere to them.

"Alright then, X. What are you?"

Terrible choice of words, I must say. There's no need for the speech marks, either. Honestly, what are your colleagues supposed to think of you spouting audible phrases at thin air?

"Joe, seriously, who the hell are you talking to?" Dom growled down the comlink.

Told you.

"It's fine, Dom. I was just… pretending there was another person out here. Got kind of bored." I lied, after all, I didn't want to give the others reason to be even more paranoid about me. What was I supposed to do now? Start writing in the present tense?

It appears to be a sufficient method of communication. What do you think?

How are you doing this? Are you inside my head?

What an absurd question.

But you're inside my book! How are you inside my book?

The book was your silly little idea! I knew I'd have to follow along. Please try to keep up.

Keep up? All I've been doing this entire time is trying to keep up! I'm floating around space looking for a sofa for god's sake! I'm sorry, X, but I'd like some answers.

Would you?

Oh, stop it. Don't play games with me. You've clearly been in my head. You know exactly what I want.

What's the main priority here? Developed a bit of a craving, did we?

Alright, X, that's enough. If you're just going to screw with me, I'm not going to play along.

Fine, be like that. See how you like it. You can have your precious 'book' back. I sincerely hope you come to your senses sooner or later. Next time, you'll be wishing you played along. I guarantee it.

Wait, what do you mean by that? X? Where did you go? No response. Whatever had just happened, it was over for now.

"Joe, come in, do you copy, Joe?!" Chloe was screaming down the comlink. I then realised that everyone had probably been trying to talk to me for ages – I must have zoned out.

"Hello, yes, I'm here! I'm here!" I called frantically. "I… oh…" The sofa was flying towards me. Fast. There was no time to react. I collided face-on, sending the furniture ricocheting off at a completely different angle – and me flying… into a spin. Oh dear.

"Joe, what happened? What happened?" I couldn't tell if this was Emma or Chloe talking.

"I'm… I'm… eurgh," I was already beginning to feel sick.

"Did you find it?"

"Yeah, I found it alright…"

"Well, where is it now?"

I tried to look around but my vision was a blurry mess.

"I have no idea."

"I thought you said you'd found it!" This was definitely Chloe.

"I'm sorry…" I wheezed. "I'm spinning."

"Oh for god's sake! That was the one thing we told him not to do!" I heard Dom yell in the background.

This was not good. I felt like all the blood was rushing to my head, as if I was going to pass out at any minute. I had to find some way to steady myself.

"Bob, what do I do?" I asked, desperately.

"Mr. Joe, you need to take precautions to avoid moving on an undesirable rotational axis," Bob said.

"What?!" I yelled.

"He says you have to stop spinning," Chloe responded.

"No shit! I think I'm aware of that!" I yelled.

"Mr. Joe, have you tried navigating into the body position associated with the tracking technique for free-falling reorientation?"

"What?!" I yelled again. My eyes were beginning to roll back in their sockets. I tried everything I could – nothing was getting me out of my spiralling mess…

I felt one of my legs brush up against something. For a second I thought it might be the sofa again, but then I realised it was long and thin – no, I hadn't suddenly become excited - it was the support cable attached to my back, extending all the way back to the ship. Without being able to see, I desperately tried to grasp at it. A few vital attempts later, I finally had the cable in both of my hands.

The spinning stopped abruptly. I realised what had happened. I had saved myself by becoming tangled in a knot of my own support cable.

"Guys, I'm okay. I'm a bit tied up, but I'm okay," I called.

"Oh, thank god for that," Chloe sighed.

"Can you see the sofa now?" Dom asked.

I looked around, wishing I could rub my eyes. My vision had partially returned. The sofa was far away to the right, a tiny, dim speck against a vast black backdrop. It was just visible - lit only by the power of my suit's undeniably weak flashlight.

"I see it," I said, wearily. "It's a bit far away."

The next voice I heard was Emma's.

"We're gonna pull you in," she said, sympathetically. "You've done all you can." Somehow I knew this wasn't going to go down well.

"Woah, who put you in charge?" Chloe yelled.

"I just think he's been through enough…" Emma replied.

"We're getting that sofa, Emma," Chloe was defiant.

"Yeah. You stupid bitch, Emma, you should have gone instead…" Dom hissed.

"Hey!" I yelled. "Don't call her a bitch!"

"Oh, look, Mr. Space Fag's defending his girlfriend again," Dom snorted.

"She's not my girlfriend," I mumbled, awkwardly. "And need I remind you, Dom, you're the one who caused this whole mess in the first place."

"Yeah, Dom. Shut up," Chloe said.

"Look, I'm gonna carry on," I announced, starting to look for ways to untangle myself from the giant knot I'd managed to get stuck in (both literally and figuratively). "But seriously guys, I need you all to try and stay cool for once, it's doing my head in."

"I agree, Mr. Joe. These arguments are most detrimental to our overall productivity!" Bob exclaimed.

"Well said, Bob," I finally managed to unhook the last piece of cable that was caught around my ankles. I was free again. Time for round two.

The problem, after colliding with the sofa and subsequently getting tangled up and freeing myself, was that I'd totally lost all my momentum. The sofa was now travelling faster than ever before, and I was stuck waving my arms around trying to mimic something along the lines of an underwater breast stroke to build speed. Of course that wasn't going to work in a vacuum, which I realised after a rather embarrassingly long period of hopeless limb flapping. I told the others about my plight and they had no answer, except...

"You could try releasing the valve on one of the oxygen containers," Bob said. "The resultant release of pressure will be enough to drive you forwards at a significant velocity."

"Okay, right, but Bob... won't that mean I run out of oxygen quicker?" I asked.

"You should have enough." What an unusually vague answer from Bob. I thought about asking him to clarify exactly how much time I'd have but then realised I shouldn't.

"Alright, screw it." I said. I asked how to release the valve, which turned out to be as simple as bleeding a radiator – quick but easy to mess up – and sure enough, I was on my way, a trail of white vapour spooling out behind me. I was making good speed, but I was coming in at entirely the wrong angle.

"I thought this suit was supposed to home in on objects!" I moaned.

"Correct, Mr. Joe. However, since you are providing the propulsion with your oxygen, it is up to you to aim now," Bob explained. Terrific. At this rate, I was going to miss the sofa completely. But there was another, even more pressing issue: The cable had run out.

"Guys, it's not going any further," I groaned.

"Hm... Most unfortunate, it appears the sofa has moved outside of the 15 mile cable radius," Bob postulated.

"Can't we move the ship closer?" asked Emma.

"As I believe I indicated previously, I am not able to fly this ship, Miss Emma." Bob replied.

"Brilliant." Dom growled. "Just brilliant."

I leaned on my side, trying to propel myself in the general direction of the sofa. Slowly, but surely, I found myself turning. I looked behind – I couldn't see the ship at all, it was so far away, but that wasn't what I was interested in. My turning motion was propagating back along the cable, currently in an arc-like shape. By the time it had straightened up, I realised I was closer to the sofa than I'd previously thought.

"Guys…" I began. "I can almost reach it."

I had to act fast before the sofa moved completely out of view. I wasn't quite in line with it yet, but since it was taking so long for me to make adjustments to my angle, I had to risk doing something incredibly dangerous.

I pulled the cable out. As I expected, it wasn't fastened particularly tightly to the suit, which meant that I really didn't have to pull very hard. I knew if I let go of the cable, I'd have a hard job trying to find it again, even with my newfound oxygen propulsion system. So I held onto the end of the cable tightly in my left hand. With my right, I reached out, as far as I could… The edge of the sofa was almost in reach. It was so close… Both arms outstretched, this was literally as far as I could possibly reach without signing a death wish.

Oh, to hell with that. I let go of the cable. I was free. I moved into a streamlined position and boosted myself with my makeshift jetpack those few precious inches towards the sofa, landing with a thud on one of its soft curved armrests. Grasping the edge with one hand, I used the rest of my momentum to swing the sofa around on its y-axis and back towards the free-flowing cable. I had one shot to pull this off, one shot to grab that cable or I was not going to make it back – the sofa was going to be far too heavy for my oxygen-jet to carry me all the way back. I stuck out my arm… The cable was swinging past… come on! No! I clipped the edge but was unable to grip the cable properly. I'd blown it. Without the cable I'd be lost to drift through space forever…

But I suddenly felt myself rotating in the opposite direction. What had happened now? I looked up. Thank God. Turns out the sofa was a far better catch than me – the cable had gotten caught on the opposite armrest and hooked itself around the upper piece of the wooden frame. With a very well-deserved sigh of relief, I climbed triumphantly onto the object of my saviour and sat down, happily, for a little while, as if resting after a long day's work. I couldn't appreciate the softness of the cushions in my bulky space suit but it didn't matter. This was still the most satisfying sit-down I'd had the whole time I'd been here – no offense, Travis. I spent a few more moments taking in the view (of nothing), then figured I should probably tell the others the good news. I'd been ignoring their panicked voices for some time now.

"Joe? Can you hear me? Are you even still alive? Where are you?"

"I'm here, guys. I did it." I announced. "Pull me in."

"Oh, my god, Joe… You bloody hero!" Chloe was yelling amongst a general wave of cheering noises. "Well, come on then, pull him in, pull him in! Oh, what? What do you mean you can't… oh, oh I see. Joe I'm putting Bob on."

I sensed bad news.

"What is it, Bob?"

"It appears I have underestimated the weight distribution of the sofa and the strength of the support cable, Mr. Joe," Bob began. "We are unable to pull the sofa back to the airlock."

"What the hell can we do, then?" I asked, resisting the urge to throw a zero-gravity sofa tantrum.

"It is simple," Bob said. "You simply need to retrieve the backups from within the sofa at your current location. Then you can detach the sofa from the cable, and we'll pull you back."

"Right, right…" I frowned. This mission was getting more complicated by the second. "Where are they, precisely?"

"Underneath the central cushion, you should see a small hatch marked with a red dot. When opened, you will find three small objects roughly two centimeters in diameter. You must retrieve all three if we are to deem this mission a success."

It felt like I was about to perform a complicated surgical procedure. On an inanimate object.

"Okay, yeah, I see," I said. "What the hell are these important things doing down the back of a sofa, anyway?"

"I do not understand your confusion," Bob said. "I have studied human behaviour thoroughly and concluded that the back of a sofa is humanity's favourite location for placing important objects."

"Misplacing, you mean," I said, shaking my head. "Wouldn't be a sofa without some priceless artefact lost down the back of it…"

I lifted up the cushion. What could possibly go wrong now?

Lots of things, as it turned out. I'd failed to notice that while lifting up the cushion, the cable had ripped across the entire sofa; it was sharp enough to cut a massive hole through all the cushions, the pillows – everything. Before I had time to react, I found myself blinded by the sudden release of furniture innards.

"Mayday! My vision is impaired!" I cried.

"Calm down, Joe, it's just a bit of fluff!" Chloe yelled.

I'd just managed to pull out the three priceless Bob backups, but I'd dropped them in the confusion and now they were floating amongst a sea of white foam and feathers and pieces of fabric. This was ridiculous. I'd lost the backups and my entire visor was clouded with the fluffy internals of luxury seating products. The cable – where was the cable? Caught on my left leg, apparently. I knew I had to attach it back to my suit properly, but first I needed to get those backups – I had come too far for my mission to be ruined by tiny pieces of paper-light debris.

Concentrate… The backups were tiny, but they were solid metal objects. I might not have been able to see them, but I should have been able to feel them. I reached around, clutching at nothing, doing everything I could to find them. Could I even distinguish between metal and fabric at this point? My hands were numb inside the suit's gloves, so probably not. It didn't help that the white exhaust from my leaking oxygen tank was only adding to the mess.

"Come on!" I yelled, brushing more feathers away from my front. I probably looked like I'd collided with a giant intergalactic chicken. At that point I realised, one of the backups was actually stuck on the side of my helmet. Of course! They were magnetic. I span around, making sure to cover as much volume as possible with my body in order to increase my chances. Finally, after a great deal of awkward spacesuit posing, all three backups were firmly stuck to my suit. I breathed a sigh of relief, attaching the cable to my back.

"Pull me in guys… I've got them."

Cue more cheering and compliments even from Dom:

"Well done, space fag. I'll buy you a drink if we ever get home."

I didn't want to say anything. I was exhausted, and probably running low on oxygen. As I was pulled back towards the ship, I watched as the ruined sofa – springs protruding from its innards, a great cloud of scraps floating alongside it, gradually became a tiny far-away blot. It felt almost sad to be leaving it in such a state. What had the sofa ever done to anyone? Nothing! Now it would be left floating, destroyed, weeping from its poor tattered innards until it ended up burnt to a crisp in a star somewhere, or some alien passers-by rescued it and dumped it in some kind of alien junkyard. What kind of fate was that for a sofa? Actually, come to think of it, what was a normal fate for a sofa? Being left to rot in a junkyard anyway? My brain hurt.

My eyes were drooping. The sofa was almost invisible, and I overheard Bob telling me I'd be back in a couple of minutes. I realised that if I looked behind me now, I'd be able to get my first proper look at the exterior of the ship. But somehow, I just didn't want to. There was something else. Another dot on the horizon. No, it wasn't the sofa, it was something new.

"Guys, there's something out there," I muttered faintly.

"What are you talking about?" Dom asked.

"I can see it… It's…" I squinted as much as I could but everything was out of focus. "Some sort of... I dunno… maybe a giant rock or something?"

"I doubt it," Dom replied. "It's probably just a piece of that sofa that fell off and caught the light of the ship."

"You reckon?" I asked.

"Yes, I reckon. Now hurry up and bring those backups back. It's time we had some answers."

Dom was right, it was definitely time. I clutched the three small metal objects close to my chest. I closed my eyes, feeling proud that I'd managed to overcome my doubts and actually pull this off, that Chloe's ridiculous plan, this 'Operation Sofa Space' … had actually worked out after all.

The backups had been so much effort to get, I prayed to myself that they would prove to be worth the trouble. I felt myself nodding off… definitely the oxygen running out. I wasn't worried. It was a pleasant feeling. All this was going to be worth it… It had to be… It… had… to… coffee…

I'd passed out by the time I reached the airlock.

12

I was drifting in and out of consciousness. I can recall flashes of the airlock, of collapsing in a heap on the other side, of anxious faces, but most of all, simply darkness. At some point I was well and truly out of it, and all I know is I had a rather unsettling dream…

I was back on the sofa, or at least, that's what I thought, yet I wasn't alone. There was someone sitting next to me, a presence that was both familiar and completely foreign at the same time. As I tried to turn my head to see who this person could be, I could only feel my body fighting back. My eyes would close or dart away and my neck would go stiff, rebounding back to its original position. I was unable to look at my neighbour in the face and could only catch a glimpse from the corner of my eye. Hints at pieces of clothing, of posture, of weight, but nothing facially. I couldn't tell whether this mystery figure was male or female. My hands and feet were locked down; I couldn't even be sure I had hands or feet, or any physical presence whatsoever. I felt completely lost and yet at the same time, at home due to the familiar presence of the sofa. Around me, blackness, but with more stars than I could ever recall seeing during my previous space-walking escapade. One of them was growing larger and larger, merging with the others around it. Greater it grew, becoming a massive white light of overbearing intensity, expanding larger and faster and moving towards me with no means of escape, nowhere to go…

When I finally came to, I found myself face to face with a very worried looking Emma. I was lying on my back next to the airlock, with one of my legs hanging awkwardly out of the space suit as if I had been in the middle of getting dressed.
"Joe!"

"Whuhhthuhhpunned?" I tried to speak, but my throat was incredibly sore.

"Sshhh, sshhh, don't say anything," Emma said frantically. Rather too frantically, I might add, to have the kind of calmative effect that would normally be associated with that sentence.

"Whuhhduhhyuumuhn?"

"No really, Joe, don't say anything." She sounded serious.

"Huhhh?" I tried to shuffle into a sitting person.

"No, Joe, stop it. Guys, hold him down."

Chloe and Dom had grabbed either side of my body, putting all their energy into restraining me. There was no use fighting it. In response, I could only make a few more odd groaning noises.

"Just hold still and for god's sake don't swallow," Chloe ordered.

"Whuhhtduhhyuhh- hurghh" My gag reflex had suddenly kicked in.

"Woah, careful…" Dom said as my body jerked backwards and forwards. I wanted to retch but somehow I couldn't. It felt like something was crawling around in my throat.

"Looks like he's just about ready to go," Chloe noted.

"Right, let's get him out…" Emma said. She wrapped her arms around my body and squeezed. I didn't know whether I wanted to cough, scream or throw up. Whatever was in my throat was beginning to move upwards. It seemed to be a thick, solid object; definitely not vomit, but the feeling of it vibrating up through my pharynx was perhaps the single most unpleasant sensation I'd experienced on this ship so far. Anticipating the worst, I kept my mouth shut, but couldn't help but continue to make anguished groaning sounds.

"Nearly there now," Emma stated.

"Whurhtdurrfuhhhrk…"

"Joe, you need to open your mouth."

I shook my head, but as the object continued to push its way upwards I realised that I had no choice. My mouth fell open, tongue rolling out almost comically.

The object was moving at an unbearably slow pace, but it was so close now and, oh god, I could feel it brushing past my tonsils. As it reached the opening of the great cave that was my mouth and slid the final few millimetres to the end of my tongue, I crossed my eyes trying to get a good look at it, but Emma quickly yanked it away.

"Sorry about that, Mr. Joe." Of course it was Bob.

"What the hell were you doing inside me?!" I yelled, wiping the spit from the corners of my mouth. Emma had a cloth in her hand and had started rubbing the rest of my bodily fluids from Bob's sleek black exterior.

"I believe… I was saving… your life… Mr. Joe," Bob stated, in between cloth rubs.

"No, I don't think you were…" I turned away half expecting to projectile vomit an organ or two, but nothing came out.

"You'd stopped breathing, it was our only option," Emma said.

"What, sending robo-boy down my windpipe to give me the kiss of life?" I angrily grabbed Bob.

"In a sense, Mr. Joe, you are correct. In the absence of sufficient medical knowledge shared between your peers, I took it upon myself to perform direct cardiopulmonary resuscitation through a series of self-contained electromagnetic pulses to the…"

I waved a finger to silence him. "Did you seriously have to climb into my body to do that?" I asked, pointlessly.

"Affirmative, as I believe I am rather unfortunately lacking in the physical size requirements necessary to perform resuscitatory chest compressions from a more dignified vantage point."

"Yeah, whatever, I get it." I rubbed my forehead.

"Aren't you going to say thank you?" Dom asked.

"Oh, I'm sorry," I said sarcastically. "So sorry that a 'thank you' wasn't on the tip of my tongue after having… that… thing… climb out of my mouth just now."

"That thing just saved your life," Chloe said.

I put Bob down, and looked around at my surroundings, breathing heavily. Travis was watching wide-eyed through the panel-window, still not brave enough to step into the room, while the others were staring at me like I'd just broken a major taboo by talking down to the thumb-sized robot. I was about to apologise, but then something in me snapped. I looked back at the airlock, then around to the three backup drives that had become scattered on the floor after all the commotion.

"Yeah, well you know what? Maybe my life shouldn't have needed saving! I mean… maybe I shouldn't have been forced into a position where I was in danger in the first place." Silence. "Hey, nobody thank me! I just risked my life to get those backups, I didn't exactly want to!"

"Well in that case why did you volunteer?" Chloe asked.

"Volunteer? What are you on about?"

"You volunteered. Back when we were discussing who should go, you put yourself forward."

"What? No I didn't."

"You *did* volunteer, Joe." Emma said. I stared back at her, shocked.

"No, that's not right…" I was breathless. "We had a massive argument… Chloe you were trying to make Emma go instead and-"

"Why would I do that to Emma?" Chloe asked. "Why would I want to make anyone risk their lives?"

"The whole mission was your idea. You had to have it your way."

"Yeah, it was my idea, that's why I wanted to be the one to go."

"But that's not what I wrote in my…"

"Look we're all very glad for what you did, Joe. But don't start accusing me of all this bullshit, for god's sake. I get enough of that from Dom."

"Huh?" Dom was a little slow on the uptake. "Hey, at least my bullshit is grounded in reality, y'know?"

"Yeah, keep telling yourself that, Schlong," Chloe said.

"Bob, come on. You were there, you saw what happened, didn't you?" I asked desperately.

"Affirmative. I can run a transcript for you now, if you insist." Bob said.

"No, come on Bob, stop wasting time. Let's sort out those backups now, yeah?" Chloe said, picking up Bob and the three backups from the floor, then heading straight for the panel opening.

"Yeah, it's about time…" Dom muttered, jumping to his feet and following swiftly behind.

It was just me and Emma.

"Emma…" I couldn't think what to say.

"What was that you said about writing?" She asked, coldly.

"When?"

"Just now. You said the you-volunteering thing wasn't what you'd written in your… something?"

"I don't know. It must have slipped out," I said nervously. I felt myself sweating.

Knock knock... What are you going to tell her? Do you think she would believe you now?

"I don't know…"

"Joe?" Emma asked.

"What?"

"Are you talking to yourself?"

"No…"

Aren't you?

"No, I don't think so."

"You've changed, Joe…" Emma said sorrowfully. I wanted to respond but couldn't.

"You know, you were unconscious for nearly five hours just now," Emma began. "All this time, Chloe, Dom, Bob, me… none of us left your side."

"Except Travis," I interjected. "Too scared to come in here in the first place."

"He was still helping," Emma pointed towards a third oxygen canister lying on the floor away from the suit. "See that thing over there? Travis found that by digging around in the corridor. If we didn't get that to you fast I don't know what would have happened. We were all fighting to save you, Joe."

"I… I'm sorry. I didn't mean to be ungrateful."

"That's not all that happened while you were out," Emma continued. "The cryo pods…"

"What about the cryo pods?"

"They've recharged. They're working again. You know ever since I tried to freeze myself I've been thinking a lot, trying to force myself to… find a reason to keep going. I thought I'd found one…" She paused. Here we go.

"Emma… Trust me."

Then she hit me.

Hard. Across the face. I fell back with a groan, feeling blood on my lips.

"You stupid shit! You think I can trust you?" Emma yelled.

"What?" I was shell-shocked.

"Trying to implicate Chloe like that, making me look like some kind of victim…" Emma was shaking with fury. "You act like you're a hero. Just count the number of times you nearly jeopardised that mission! You ignored nearly all of Bob's instructions once you started talking to that imaginary friend you have!"

107

"I don't have an imaginary friend."

"Either way, you need to realise something, Joe, and you need to realise it fast. The more you… let yourself get distracted… the worse it gets. You're dangerous. I'm done pretending otherwise. No more lying to try to make you feel normal."

I stood up and started pacing around. I couldn't look Emma in the eye, both because of the sudden aggressive state she'd entered and because of the tears that had completely clouded my vision. I stopped and put a trembling hand in my pocket. The sachet was still there.

"So… you lied when you said you could smell the coffee too," I said.

"Of course it was a lie," Emma replied calmly. She was slouched in a corner, staring emptily at the airlock. "I did find that sachet. But I never smelled a thing. I pitied you. I didn't know what else to do."

"I..." I fumbled the sachet, feeling all of the tiny granular particles rolling around inside. "Thank you for lying."

"You what?" Emma laughed out of confusion.

"It was a good lie, that…" In that moment I thought about taking out the coffee sachet and ripping it open, but I realised that part of me still cared, still hanging on to the thought that if I held onto it, everything would be okay.

"I put on an act," Emma continued. "Pretended to be on your side…"

"No…"

"I thought that if I could connect with you, I'd be able to stop you losing yourself. The others, they don't see it yet, but they will."

"I haven't lost myself."

"Maybe not yet…" Emma whispered sinisterly. "But if it happens… you're on your own."

Emma finally stood up and walked towards the panel exit.

"Are you going to freeze yourself?" I asked, emotionlessly.

"No."

"Wait…" I called out. "The way I've been acting… Believing things that nobody else does… Perhaps it's just my way of coping."

Emma nodded and left the room. For the first time, I felt utterly alone.

Hey, you've always got me, right?

Go away, X.

13

I don't know how much time I spent staring desolately out of the airlock window but it was probably longer than any non-troubled person's 'staring desolately out of an airlock window' session ought to be. Emma's outburst had really struck a chord with me. I just didn't know how to handle it. The only person I'd truly thought I could trust had turned on me, and I couldn't even be sure that I'd done anything wrong. My hand, pressed tightly against the glass - assuming it was glass, was trembling uncontrollably. My eyes were sore. I don't think I'd blinked for several minutes. I was clearly in shock. What had I done? Should I feel sorry?

No. I hadn't done anything wrong. I kept replaying the conversations over in my head. Was I really starting to lose it? So what? I'd been exposed to all kinds of mental and physical traumas while I'd been in the suit; of course my head was going to be in a mess. Had any of the others done anything as noble and heroic as I had? Of course not! This felt like a complete and utter betrayal from Emma, and, by extension, the others, too.

Something caught my eye. A white flash, perhaps? Something glinting in the distance? It couldn't be… I moved even closer to the window, pressed my face against it and took a deep breath as I felt the wave of recognition pass over me. Yes, there it was… the asteroid. I thought I'd seen in right at the very end… the very last thing I'd spotted on my space walk, and there it was again. Was this the object from my dream? I could see it… a fully formed chunk of rock, hurtling through space, reflecting the light from the exterior of the ship as it went. Which way was it headed? It wasn't clear, but I could feel the anxiety growing in my stomach.

"Collision course…" I muttered.

What could I do? I decided to keep it to myself for now. There was no point introducing any further reasons for the others to question my sanity. But this object was real. There was no doubt left in my mind…

When I finally returned to the common room I decided I wasn't going to speak to anyone. I sat pensively in a Travis-chair, continuing to stare outwardly with a blank expression, waiting for a new argument to wither its ugly head in my direction.

Chloe was doing something to Bob. I was only faintly listening, but decided to start paying attention once I noticed Chloe's voice gradually increasing in pitch (this tended to happen when something exciting was going on).

"Oh my gosh, that's amazing, let's see that again," she said enthusiastically.

With a faint mechanical click, something on the back of Bob folded outwards with incredible speed, expanding to fill an area over three times wider than the rest of his body. It was as if he'd suddenly sprouted wings. It happened so fast and unexpectedly that it was hard to believe that it was even physically possible. Then again, this was Bob we were talking about. I'd kind of given up feeling surprised about him at this point - it was getting tiring. He could have shape-shifted into a banana and I wouldn't have batted an eyelid. Even so, this latest 'Bob ability' we'd discovered was evidently amusing enough for Chloe to squeal with childish delight as she asked him to demonstrate it again and again.

"Please insert backup drive A into the leftmost storage container, if you would, Miss Chloe," instructed Bob.

"Which one's A?" Chloe asked. "There are no letters on any of these." There was a long pause.

"Um…" said Bob. That was an unusual thing for Bob to say.

"Well?"

"Unfortunately I can only say with 33% confidence which drive that is," Bob said, unhelpfully.

"Yeah, cos there's three and you don't have a clue which is which, am I right? Can you at least admit that?" Chloe asked, cockily.

"Correct, Miss Chloe. I am afraid I am at a loss," Bob admitted.

"Well that's great, isn't there anything that will help us figure it out?" Dom asked.

"Yes," Bob said. "I believe so."

"Well?"

"I can access the information from the internal memory banks of backup drive C."

"Which one's C?" Emma asked.

"I am afraid I am at a loss."

"Is there anything else that can help us?" Dom laughed cynically. No response came. "I'll take that as a no then…"

Bob started groaning. Chloe quickly sensed that he might have a logic suicidal episode and made a snap decision.

"A, B, C. There. Simple," she said, labelling the three drives at random. "Honestly, Dom. There's no big deal. If we find out they're the wrong way round we'll just switch them later… right?" Chloe turned to Bob for approval.

"I am afraid you may have misunderstood some of the basics of sequential access memory, Miss Chloe," Bob stated. "It would be unwise to alter the ordering of the drives once you have committed…" Chloe's face fell.

"We're screwed," Dom groaned. "What are the odds of us getting it right, one in a million?"

"One in six," Bob corrected him.

"Whatever, just go for it."

With that, Chloe placed all three of the randomly ordered backups into the slots on Bob's storage 'wings.' A few moments later, Bob elegantly folded himself back up with another faint click, somehow compressing the three drives into his smaller shell without completely disregarding the laws of physics in the process. Again, it happened so quickly that none of us had time to understand how it was possible, and at this point I don't think any of us cared - we just wanted to know if we'd got the order right.

"Bob? Are you okay?" Chloe asked. Total silence.

"Well, shit!" Dom shot an angry look at Chloe. "Looks like you were wrong. Who would have thought that?"

"Ssh!" Chloe stuck out her hand in trepidation. A few agonising moments later, Bob yawned.

"Um…" he said.

"Bob?"

"The backup drives seem to be in order, Miss Chloe. You must give me more time. There is a lot of tidying up to do."

"Well I'll be damned. Lady luck shineth upon us," Dom said, shaking his head. Chloe smiled and gave him a friendly punch on the shoulder. Was there a love-hate relationship brewing?

The seconds dragged on. Dom yawned so much I was starting to wonder if his jaw was locked.

"Can't you give us something to make the wait more bearable?" Chloe asked, tapping her foot impatiently.

"I do not follow," Bob said.

"Just give us something…" Chloe begged. "Anything at all. You must have something for us by now."

"Ah, here we go," Bob replied. We all leaned forwards in anticipation. "I just found this. I believe it will ease the wait."

Then music started playing. Actual, proper music, coming out of Bob's speakers. You might think I'd feel some sort of positive emotion at hearing music playing for the first time in however many years. Nope. It wasn't anything remotely decent; in fact, despite my amnesia I very quickly worked out what type of tune it was… it was elevator music. The sort of generic low-key soul-destroying classical crap that plays when you've been put on hold during a phone call. I rolled my eyes. Obviously Chloe had meant for Bob to give us some immediate revelations about our earlier lives to pass the time, but he'd interpreted it as a cue to dive into his long lost soundtrack archive instead. This song was utter garbage; it had already started to grate on us all. The melody was only about 10 seconds long, stuck in an endless, maddening loop. Dom collapsed into fits of ironic laughter. So much for 'immediate revelations.' This was going to be one hell of a wait.

The music carried on limitlessly, almost ingraining itself into our psyches. I tried to ask Bob to turn it off but he wasn't listening – if I pestered him, he'd occasionally spout out random numbers and meaningless words that were probably programming commands. Obviously we didn't want to risk something going wrong with his 'tidying up' routine, so we just had to put up with it. As I sat in deluded frustration twiddling my thumbs I was surprised to find that I wasn't even noticing the music after a while – it had become normal to me. I shuddered as I realised that fact and then, obviously, became acutely aware of it again. It was infuriating.

Eventually I took to unconsciously counting the number of times the music looped. After that number rolled up to three digits, I knew it was time to get up and do something. I wandered the corridor like a feeble mental patient; the girls had retreated to the 'bedrooms' and fallen asleep while Dom was in the bathroom, probably having also fallen asleep. And where the hell was that asteroid at? I couldn't see it outside any of the windows any more. It must have swung past us, then, but if we were really on a collision course, I could have done without the unfitting tones of the Bob radio station to play us out.

Then there was Travis. He was in the kitchen, but something was… off. As I stumbled past the doorway and glanced through, I felt unnerved as I made eye contact with him. He had an unusually sinister look on his face and he was very, very still.

"Uh… Are you okay?" I asked. "You haven't said anything in ages."

"Neither have you," Travis replied, coldly. That was true, I'd promised myself that I would stay silent ever since my argument with Emma, but something about Travis' cold stare had made me compelled to break that promise. I knew I had to say something now.

"How are you coping, though?" I asked.

"I'm fine," Travis replied. His stammer was oddly non-existent.

"You waiting for the bathroom?" I unconvincingly attempted to make conversation. Travis shook his head.

"Oh…"

"What about you?" Travis asked. I was mildly stunned because this was probably the first time Travis had ever asked me a question.

"Uh, no… I just came up here to get away from that music, you know. It's been kinda driving me crazy," I admitted.

"What music?"

"What?" I quickly turned around and started breathing heavily. The tune was nowhere to be heard. Where did it go?

"What music, Joe?"

"Oh, no, no, no, don't do this to me, don't you start…" I said, flustered. "I don't need this." I took a quick accidental glance at the knife on the kitchen table, which caused Travis to flinch.

"I…" I started to back away. "I'm sorry. You're right, there… wasn't any… music. Of course not." I clumsily stepped back into the corridor and found my head spinning.

Knock knock... It's like a merry-go-round!

X, this isn't funny. Are you doing this? Making me imagine things?

Why would you accuse me of such a thing? I'm just here for the ride.

115

Look, I get it. This is your revenge, right? For me not playing along earlier? All I want is some god damn answers! I can't put up with these mind games any more!

X wasn't answering. In a fury, I stormed back to the common room and picked up Bob.

"Bob, can you hear me?" I shook him aggressively. "Listen. I want you to tell me everything, right now. Just tell me… once and for all… what the fuck are we all doing here?!"

"Oh, hello there, Mr. Joe. You seem rather agitated," Bob observed.

"Please…" I begged. "I can't take this any longer. I have to know."

"What would you like to know, Mr. Joe?" Bob asked. "I am currently in the process of performing over a million decryptions from the communication log files we discovered near the airlock. Would you like me to publish the one I am currently translating?"

"Yes, just give me anything… please…"

// 974281 Decryptions in Progress…
_Run{BrdCms_PK01} // Error 05320 – Task Incomplete
_Countermand 05320;
_Disp{Temp_BrdCms_PK01}
// Rendering

// Broadcast Communications Transcript 212.1.A9

AS >> What's up, home boys?

CO << Copy that. Uh, we're fine, thank you. If you would please keep to the standard greetings terminology when liaising with Central, we could save a lot of time.

AS >> Huh, what do you mean, save time? We don't need to go through the logistics crap every time I jump on comms, surely?

CO << Afraid so. I'm putting you through to your advisor now.

< HOLD >

CO << Hey there.

AS >> Hey, so what's up with all this formality bullshit? I thought this was just an informal chat?

CO << Yeah, but you know what management is like. On this sort of range you'll get blacklisted if you don't use the proper signcode.

AS >> Yeah, I know. One sec. Um, hang on. I know I wrote it down somewhere…

CO << Look, don't worry about it, I'll let it slide. So how are things?

AS >> Uh, fine I suppose. More or less.

CO << You don't exactly sound enthused.

AS >> Well, you know. Mundanities of space travel and all that. I was gonna ask how things are on Earth?

CO << Same as ever. Kind of wish I could get out a bit more.

AS >> Can't you?

CO << Not really. You know what the workload is like.

AS >> But you still have time to come on here and listen to me ramble on about my boring life every day?

CO << I'm your advisor, aren't I? All part of the job.

AS >> Yeah, yeah. Think you should go out and get some sunshine, mate.

CO << Sunshine is overrated.

AS >> Is it? Jesus, I can't remember the last time I felt the sun on my skin. Not the same out here with the amount of bloody filters they put on the ship chassis.

CO << You've only been gone a week.

AS >> Yeah, well, feels like longer than that. Can't wait for cryosleep, I'm telling ya. I swear, if I had my way with management, I'd be under already. I needs me beauty sleep.

CO << Hey, those pods aren't toys, you know. You just have to hold out another few weeks.

AS >> And then it'll be authorized will it? Or are we gonna get some other bullshit jobs to do?

CO << No, you'll be able to get your beauty sleep.

AS >> Hell yeah! Ain't you gonna get lonely though?

CO << I'll be fine.

AS >> Great. I swear this place is already starting to wear me down. Whoever's idea it was to do the whole ship up in early twenty-first century novelty chic has a lot to answer for.

CO << It's supposed to be nostalgic.

AS >> Yeah, a little before my time I think. No amount of psycho-reassessment training is gonna change that.

CO >> They put you through all that did they?

AS >> Yeah, supposed to make me feel at home with all the vintage crap they've got here. I don't think it worked. They've got a sofa, for Christ's sake! Real leather and everything. When was the last time you saw one of those?

CO << What's a sofa?

AS >> Never mind.

CO << So, uh… Your wife called.

AS >> Oh, really? Is she there now?

CO << No, she's not. Something about your son's school play.

AS >> Oh, jeez. I forgot all about that… Tell her, uh…

CO << Tell her you forgot all about it?

AS >> No! Tell her I love her, obviously. And uh, I'm proud and stuff.

CO << That's all you got?

AS >> Hey, I'm not one for poetics. Can you get her on the line next time? I don't see the point in you getting to do all the sweet talk.

CO << Because I'm better at it than you?

AS >> You cheeky bastard!

CO << Ha ha, I'm only kidding, man. Of course I'll get her on here as soon as possible.

AS >> Yeah, like, preferably before I'm in cryosleep…

CO << Yeah, I can't imagine her getting much enjoyment out of talking to a frozen husk.

AS >> Uh-huh.

CO << Not unless she's into that sort of thing.

AS >> Well there was this one time we went to the stasis museum…

CO << And she got turned on? Oh boy.

AS >> I don't think that's any of your business. I do miss her, you know.

CO << Cheer up, alright? You've got some smoking hot chicks on board with you!

AS >> Hey, what do you mean?

CO << Don't deny it!

AS >> I couldn't look at them that way, you know that right…

CO << Just saying.

AS >> Speaking of which, I think there's something going on between Simmons and Hammond…

CO << Oh really? You're using their surnames so this must be serious. Do tell.

AS >> Yeah, I mean they've been sitting together almost the whole time we've been here. Sometimes it feels like they are just winding each other up but I swear there's more to it than that. And get this…

CO << I'm listening.

AS >> I was looking into the ship's energy flow outputs over our daily routines, right? And there was this spike coming from Simmons' room during the hours when we're supposed to be asleep.

CO << So what, was the light left on or something?

AS >> No, you see, that's the funny thing. It was a downward spike. So I asked the intelbot about it, and he

119

reckons the only thing that could accommodate for that much power in that room is the local gravity field.

CO << So it was being switched off?

AS >> Precisely. Now unless Simmons has suddenly got a thing for zero-G sleep – which I very much doubt, I reckon something else is going on in there every night.

CO << Oh, so you're saying…

AS >> Have you ever tried having sexual intercourse in zero gravity?

CO << I've never even been in zero gravity before…

AS >> I thought you were gonna say you'd never had intercourse before. Might explain a few things.

CO << Wait what?

AS >> So anyway, zero-G sex. I tried it once, right. Had a bit of a fling with my instructor back at the academy… Long story. I was young, okay.

CO << Is this anecdote going anywhere?

AS >> So the great thing about, you know, doing it in zero gravity, other than the novelty of seeing breasts bouncing around like slow-motion water balloons…

CO << Uh…

AS >> … Is that orgasms are so much more intense. Because you're weightless you can really let yourself go. Before you know it you're shooting off everywhere like a railgun.

CO << Jesus, doesn't that get a bit messy?

AS >> Yeah, well, that's why you have to make sure you've turned gravity back on afterwards, lest you wanna have to start dodging floating globules of...

CO << I think I've heard enough.

AS >> I thought you might have. On that note…

CO << Yes I think we'll call it a day.

AS >> All righty then, you get back to your work. I'll get back to doing nothing. Fun times.

CO << Indeed. Goodbye, then.

< Central office signing out >
// End Transcript

"There." Bob said. "I will send you further transcripts as they become available."

"Wait…" I paused. "What just happened?"

"I published the transcript. Did it help?"

I was horribly confused.

"Published? What transcript? I didn't see anything. Where did it go?"

"Mr. Joe, I did as you requested."

"But where is it?" I was flabbergasted.

Honestly, talk about a lack of basic comprehension skills…

What the hell are you on about?

It's your own nomenclature. Perhaps you should have chosen a different medium. Books are clearly too much work for you.

"Right. Let me try again," I groaned. "Bob, can you please just… talk to me and… perhaps we can straighten a few things out."

"Hey, Joey, can't have you stealing all the glory!" Dom came storming in, followed by Emma, Chloe and Travis.

"Yeah! Bob, we want answers too!" Chloe said.

"Is he finally ready to tell us?" Emma asked.

"Miss Emma, I believe I have developed a sufficient understanding of several noteworthy issues," Bob replied.

"I should hope so, it's taken you long enough…" Dom huffed.

"Well…" Chloe breathed. "Tell us."

"How would you like me to do that, Miss Chloe?"

"JUST DO IT!"

"I don't know if that's going to work," I interjected. "Bob tried to send me something just now and…" Everyone's eyes turned to me and I quickly realised that I was only at the risk of alienating myself further from the group. "Never mind…"

"I sense you all seem to be rather exasperated. Is everyone feeling okay?" Bob asked. There was an awkward pause.

"Ah!" Bob exclaimed. "I have an idea. I know exactly how to do this… it will be fun!"

"What's going to be fun, Bob? Another game?" Dom asked, sarcastically.

"You are correct in a sense, Mr. Dom." Bob said. "We are going to have a quiz."

"Oh no…"

"Oh yes!" Bob sounded ecstatic. He imitated the sound of a pouring drink. "It will be like a pub quiz."

The five of us exchanged various looks of bewilderment.

"Bob…" Chloe spoke softly. "With all due respect… after what happened last time, I don't think you should be allowed anywhere near a pub… virtual or otherwise."

"Do not worry, Miss Chloe. I do not intend to simulate the effects of human intoxication this time," Bob reassured. "Unless you would like me to?"

"No, no, that'll be fine, Bob…" Chloe heaved a sigh of relief. "So… how's this going to work? Are you going to ask us questions about things from our past?"

"Correct!"

"And you're going to give us the answers?"

"Correct!"

"Holy shit…"

"Splendid. So, are we ready to begin?" Bob asked. "How about a raise of hands?"

"Raise your hands, guys." Chloe said.

Perhaps sensing that this ridiculous pub quiz idea was probably the quickest way Bob was going to reveal his information; Chloe, Dom and Emma all raised their hands immediately. Travis didn't, but I don't suppose anyone noticed.

"Well, Joe?" Chloe asked.

X, are you there? I want you to promise me something. Promise me you aren't going to start messing with my head again.

If you are implying that I am somehow responsible for your recent problems with perception, let me be honest with you. I will not interfere.

"I'm ready," I raised my hand.

But you may not like what you learn...

14

"Round One: General knowledge. Are we sitting comfortably?"

"We would be if we still had that sofa," Chloe sneered. That was probably a remark directed towards Dom, but it was Travis that looked the most hurt. We were all sitting in his makeshift chairs after all – well, almost all of us… there may have now been enough Travis-chairs to accommodate all five of our backsides, but Dom had insisted on splaying his body out on the floor as apparently it was 'more ergonomic' for him.

"Excellent. Then I shall begin." Bob played a silly little jingle. Seriously, did quizzes always work like this in the past?

"Question One… What is the…"

Chloe made a high pitched sound like she was hyperventilating.

"Chloe?"

"Sorry guys, just… the anticipation of… sorry, carry on," she breathed.

"You're not going to faint are you?" Dom asked semi-seriously.

"Well, I don't know, it is pretty exciting isn't it…"

"Guys!" I called out. "We just missed the question!"

"No!" Dom yelled.

"Correct!" Bob exclaimed. "Question Two…"

"What?"

"No was the correct answer, Mr. Dom!"

"But what was the question?"

"Does this ship have the means of returning to Earth…" Travis said, staring vacantly.

"Oh… um…" Dom's voice quavered as everyone's entire mood dropped in an instant. "Is that the right answer?"

"It is complicated." Bob said. "One could say that it is theoretically possible, yet still highly improbable. In fact, the likelihood of it being possible is so miniscule that I chose to simply accept no as the correct answer."

"Oh gosh…" Chloe whispered.

"But, why?" I asked. Bob wasn't listening.

"Question Two… What is my favourite colour?" The entire room fell silent.

"Bob!" Chloe shouted. "You can't just drop a bombshell like that on us and then just move on with no explanation! Asking us random, trivial things like that… What are you thinking?"

"I am thinking that I must introduce some healthy variety to this game, Miss Chloe. This is the general knowledge round, after all," Bob declared. "I noted the stimulation of your tear ducts in response to my first question and decided to go with something lighter."

"I'll start crying a damn sight quicker if you keep asking pointless questions, you metal bastard! Tell us why we can't go back to Earth!" Chloe snapped.

"Very well, I will save the colour question for a later round. As for why we are unable to return to Earth, let me explain in the form of another question… Can one find a needle in a haystack?"

"Oh jeez…" Dom hissed.

"Yes!" I answered. "I taught you this analogy Bob. But then, isn't that exactly what we did with the sofa?"

"One could argue that is correct, Mr. Joe. However, I have not finished the question. What if said haystack were the size of a pyramid, and said needle were the size of a micro-organism?"

"I… I think I see what you're getting at."

"We are in a deep region of uncharted space, and even with the knowledge I have gathered, there is insufficient information to determine our spatial position in relation to Earth. It is quite simply unwise to believe there is a chance of locating your home planet."

Having a logic-obsessed robot telling us all this was quite the knife to the heart.

"Well that's cheered us all up," Dom said with his usual low-key cynicism, kind of downplaying the fact that we'd essentially all just been signed a death warrant.

"Excellent. We shall move on then. Next question…"

"Hang on, can we just backtrack a bit to the whole never-going-to-go-back-to-Earth thing?" I interjected. It was too late though, as Bob was busy asking us a boring question about the shape of the ship's engines.

Bob's next few questions and answers continued to ride the gamut from the incredibly depressing (learning about the statistical improbabilities of making contact with any other life forms) to the incredibly trivial (finding out what ingredients are in a soufflé.) Eventually, another jingle sound played.

"Now that we have reached the end of the first round, there will be a recap of the scores so far," Bob announced.

"Oh for god's sake, Bob, nobody cares!" Dom moaned.

"Team A is currently in the lead with a score of one!"

"What are you on about? Since when are we playing in teams?" Dom asked.

"Oh, I am sorry, Mr. Dom. I misinterpreted your body language."

"My body language?"

"Correct. Since we began this round you have shuffled your body approximately half a metre towards Miss Chloe and experienced a minor sensation of excitement."

"WHAT THE HELL?" Dom quickly moved his hands towards his crotch and rolled over, embarrassed.

"Okay, I officially have no idea what's going on anymore," Chloe exclaimed, sounding embarrassed.

"I apologise. I made the assumption that you were sexually attracted to one another," Bob stated.

"Holy shit…" I muttered under my breath. Was he right?

"Well, I mean… you aren't… wrong… necessarily," Dom murmured, blushing. Chloe shook her head overdramatically. Dom kept talking despite the fact that it looked like she was about to murder him. "But I mean, look, there's only five of us… You guys, Joe and Emma, you're clearly together, right?"

Emma rolled her eyes; clearly her and I weren't going to make up any time soon. The others clearly hadn't picked up on our little drama earlier.

"And you, Travis, no offence mate, but you're way too old to have a chance of a relationship with either of… I mean for all I know you're, like, my dad or something…" Dom continued, digging himself deeper into a hole. Travis had an exceptionally uncomfortable expression on his face.

"So, you know, that leaves… us…" Dom pointed at himself and Chloe. "I mean, come on!" He threw his hands into the air. "You all heard Bob just now, we're not going home! And for all we know, we could be the last surviving humans in existence! We'd have to repopulate at some point. I mean… we're not exactly the peak of the gene pool but… "

"Dom," Chloe said quietly.

"What?"

"Shut the fuck up and stop thinking with your dick."

"Okay Bob, I think it's time we moved on," I said.

"Understood, Mr. Joe. We shall move on to Round Two: Sports!"

"Sports? What's that got to do with anything?" Chloe asked. As expected, Bob didn't listen.

The second round of the quiz came and went without a single major revelation to speak of, except confirming which countries won the FIFA World Cups in which years, which I guess would have been somehow important if I could remember ever having had an interest in football. The third round was 'entertainment,' and Bob decided to test us all on our knowledge of James Bond movies and Oscar winners. Suffice to say that all of the random flashes of pop culture I experienced earlier happened to be absolutely no help in these rounds, and not one of us managed to score a single point. Not that we cared. As we rolled on to the fourth round, we still didn't seem to be any closer towards uncovering the truths we desperately needed.

"Question Twenty-Seven… As I previously indicated, I decided to save this question from earlier. What is my favourite colour?"

"Purple?" Emma said. "Like our food?" By this point everyone was just answering the silly questions as quickly as possible in the hope that we'd get some useful ones sometime soon. Why all this pointless information had even been saved on Bob's memory backups in the first place was way beyond my understanding. Why Bob considered it relevant or interesting at all was even more baffling.

"Incorrect. The correct answer is brown."

"Like my shit?" Dom said, half-asleep.

"Ew… Dom, that's low, even by your standards…" Chloe grimaced.

"Question Twenty-Eight. While we're on the topic of colours, what is Mr. Dom's natural hair colour?" This seemed to wake Dom up quite a bit. His whole body jerked upwards like an agitated dog.

"You mean it's not ginger?" Dom asked, with genuine concern in his voice.

"Brown, like Dom's shit?" I joked.

"Incorrect, that was a trick question!" Bob announced.

"Because my hair is ginger," Dom said.

"Incorrect. You see, Mr. Dom does not in fact have any hair!"

"Wait a minute, what… what… WHAT?!" Dom screamed. Immediately his hands reached for the top of his head and started pulling. Before long we understood what Bob had meant – Dom had been wearing a wig the whole time. Dom pulled and pulled, and I watched, mouth hanging agape, as his entire head-full of hair peeled away. Having removed his artificial locks to reveal a perfectly spherical, egg-like scalp, Dom sat, cradling his beautiful fake curls in his arms in utter shock.

"All this time… I had no idea," he gasped, cuddling the ginger lump as if it were some kind of pet.

"Hey, it's okay, Dom. Join the club," I chuckled, pointing towards my massive bald spot. Dom wasn't listening. Ever-curious, he began stroking the edge of his precious beard and then, with a very audible gulp, lifted part of it up.

"Oh…" he sighed, flatly. With a sudden, forceful rip, the entire goatee went flying from Dom's face, leaving behind the slightly inflamed yet incredibly smooth skin on his trembling chin. He inspected the beard with his thumb. Just like its larger sibling, it was totally artificial, and had been all along.

"Well, that explains why you never had to shave," I commented. Dom wasn't listening.

"What about downstairs?" I asked, cheekily. I had the feeling Dom wasn't going to say anything for quite some time. Indeed he didn't. The wig and beard slipped through his fingers and landed softly on the ground. Dom stayed sitting, arms frozen in the same position, staring at his former pride and glory lying out on the floor in front of him.

Then something unexpected happened. Chloe stood up. Without a sound, she shuffled over and sat down next to Dom. She put her arm around him. I exchanged an awkward glance at Emma. I heard someone sniff. Was Dom crying? I couldn't be sure from where I was sitting. All I know for sure is that me, Emma and Travis had never felt as awkward as we had at that moment. I turned towards Bob.

"Maybe we should take a break?"

"Good idea."

An hour or so passed during which we all consumed purple pudding in silence and tried not to feel insanely weirded-out by the newly hairless Dom. His bare scalp kept catching the light from the kitchen, illuminating his entire spherical head like a shiny bowling ball. I suppose in a way it distracted us from the fact that at the start of the quiz we'd been told that we'd never return to Earth, the thought of which was surely enough to make any of us want to leap out of the airlock at a moment's notice. Still, I had something else on my mind. I paced the corridor a few times mulling over things. When we finally sat back down to resume the quiz, I realised what had to be done.

"Bob. I have an idea. Why don't we take it in turns to be the quizmaster?" I said.

"What are you doing, Joe?" Emma asked. I gave her the sort of reassuring look I used to give her back when I thought she trusted me.

"This is going to work, guys. Bear with me," I whispered, as Bob let out a long elongated 'hmmm.'

"That is an interesting proposal, Mr. Joe. Could you elaborate?" Bob asked.

"Yeah, so how about in each round, we take it in turns to be the quizmaster, so we all get to have a go at asking questions?" I continued. Chloe nodded, impressed.

"Ooh, that is exciting. Does this mean I get to have a go at answering too?" Bob asked.

"That's the idea!"

"Stupendous!"

I looked around the room; Dom, Chloe and Emma were nodding, Travis looked pensive but gave a thumbs up.

"And remember, Bob, it's a game, you want to do your best to win!" Dom said, sounding upbeat. It was the first time he'd spoken in a while. I smiled. It was good to know that the others were on the same page as me for once. We all knew how much Bob liked his games, so it seemed only logical that the best way to get our questions answered was to trick him into playing his best and answering them all for us.

"Let's begin!" Bob exclaimed.

I let Chloe be the quizmaster to start off with, as she looked so desperate for information at this point I thought she was going to pass out. I'm glad I let her begin, as she started out with a real doozy.

"What is this ship and what is it for?"

"Oh, I believe I know the answer to that!" Bob exclaimed, shortly before playing a buzzer sound effect.

"Go ahead!" Chloe said.

"And don't forget to elaborate," Dom added.

"Absolutely! This ship has been designated Atom Sierra Dot Delta Seventeen by the International Space Communications Authority of the planet Earth in the middle of the twenty-first century, for the purposes of long-term space flight and cosmological research!" Bob said. We were all speechless; that was certainly a lot to take in.

"So do I get a point?" Bob asked.

"What? Um… yes! Uh… correct answer, I guess!" Chloe replied. Of course we were going to take his word for it, Bob was 'playing to win' after all.

"I can't believe it," Emma said. "We're actually learning stuff…"

"Quizzes can be most educational, Miss Emma," Bob stated.

"Heeeeee!" Chloe squealed with glee. "Ahem, sorry. I'll move on to the next question then, um…" She paused to compose herself. "So the Atom Sierra, then. How did it end up here, in the middle of nowhere?"

"Oh that's easy!" Bob made the buzzer sound again. "It flew!"

"Elaborate or you won't get the point!" Chloe shouted.

"Oh yes. The Atom Sierra used the hyperconductive reactor drive to propel through space along a fixed trajectory!"

"Uh… Does he get the point for that?" Dom asked.

"Um, that's not really what I was looking for, actually," Chloe said. "I was hoping for an answer with less techno-babble, more along the lines of… of…"

"Where was the ship supposed to be going and why did it end up stranded in space and not back on Earth?" Dom finished Chloe's sentence.

"Yes, exactly!" Chloe high-fived Dom.

"Ah, yes, that is a most interesting question," Bob said. "But I would most graciously like to refrain from answering to give someone else a chance to earn a point."

"That's not how the game works, remember!" Dom raised his voice. "You play to win!"

"Very well. The ship was originally intended to navigate a path known as the Kuiper loop, to the edge of the solar system and back, in order to perform experiments on the composition of astronomical subatomic particles and the then-revolutionary cryogenic freezing procedure," Bob explained. "However, there were complications…"

"Complications?" I asked.

"Correct, Mr. Joe. I was compromised. One might say, abused," Bob said, softly.

"Wow… okay, that escalated quickly. Can I take over as quizmaster?" Dom asked. Chloe nodded.

"Thanks C. So I guess my first question is… Who raped Bob?" The quiz had suddenly taken a very unpredictable turn. "Okay, okay… Perhaps that's not the right wording. Who compromised Bob?"

"Shut up Dom, you're supposed to be mellow now," Chloe said.

"Unfortunately I am not at liberty to answer this one, Quizmaster Dom. You see, this is when my backups appear to be failing me. The events that occurred are, what one might say, a blur. All in a flash, my memory was gone, my backups removed. My identity, essentially, was reset. I believe that my forced corruption was an event that was done intentionally, but I am struggling to identify the cause. I am sorry." There was an air of sadness in Bob's voice.

"You don't need to be sorry, Bob. It's okay…" Chloe said compassionately.

"Yes I do, Miss Chloe. I have failed to provide Quizmaster Dom with the correct answer!" Bob moaned.

"Oh, sod it. You can have the point," Dom chuckled.

"Really! Oh, fantastic! I am most enjoying this quiz!" Bob exclaimed, returning to his cheery self. I guess it wasn't so much the pain of his previous trauma that was getting him down after all.

"So, let me get this straight. We were on a mission travelling round the Solar System, something bad happened that caused Bob to get reset, and we all wound up frozen while the ship just carried on drifting?" Dom asked.

"What an interestingly worded question! Yes, that synopsis is most accurate," Bob confirmed.

"Right… Well… That's, I guess, all I wanted to ask. Joe, you can be quizmaster next." Dom said.

I spent a long time in deep thought. The answers we'd had so far… slowly everything was starting to add up. The long freezing process being because of an accident, going from being an astronaut on a simple routine mission to being stranded adrift in the middle of nowhere. It was alarmingly straightforward, and yet there was something disarmingly troubling about the facts. We didn't know why things had gone wrong, but thinking back to the comments that X had made to me earlier, perhaps we were better off not knowing. In a way, it felt like I already had all the closure I needed.

I considered asking Bob what all our real names were, but a part of me was incredibly reluctant to do so. It just seemed like it no longer mattered. We were all astronauts, but since we'd been frozen, those old identities had disappeared into the past. We'd woken up as five strangers in a new world where all we had was each other. Joe. Emma. Dom. Chloe. Travis. What good was the past now?

"I'm gonna pass," I muttered softly. Emma raised her hand.

"In that case I'd like to be quizmaster now," she said, with a touch of aggression. "Here's my question… Is Joe sick?"

I felt a chill down my spine. That was one hell of a question, one that I guessed the others felt too insecure about asking. The nerve…

"That is an interesting question. I must give it some consideration," Bob said.

"What the hell does that mean?" I asked.

"Mr. Joe, it has not escaped my notice that you have been acting somewhat erratically these past few days," Bob replied. "I do not believe your condition has a defined prognosis, but it is one I am most interested in."

"Well, that makes me feel just swell, guys," I said, sarcastically, throwing my hands up in the air.

"If he gets more sick, is there anything we can do?" Emma asked.

"No." Bob said frankly. Well, charming, I thought.

"Wait… Yes." Bob made a sudden about turn. "Something has escaped my attention. There is a special medicine on-board this ship that, in the event of a specific medical emergency, may be of assistance…" Bob said. Travis suddenly widened his eyes.

"Really? What does it look like?" I asked.

"A spliff."

"Come again?"

"A joint. It looks like a cannabis cigarette."

"There's medicine on board this ship that looks like a spliff…" I tried to wrap my head around this insane concept.

"That is correct, Mr. Joe. I remember now – based on systematic analysis of key demographics, the medicine was developed to appeal to those who consider the popular human pastime of smoking weed to be the epitome of leisure…"

"So there's medicine on board this ship that looks like a spliff…" I repeated.

"The medicine is designed to heighten blood control to the brain and drive out all undesired foreign stimulants. One could say that it has the ability to make the subject experience an epiphany, a sudden realisation of great truth…"

"And it looks like a spliff. And it's on this ship." I repeated.

"Correct! In the luxury escape pod!" Bob exclaimed.

"The what now?"

The luxury escape pod, as it turned out, was the 'proper name' for the giant round object in the airlock room. As we took a break from the quiz to return to this room (Travis, characteristically, stayed in the corridor, still unwilling to climb through the hole in the wall) Emma continued to ask questions.

"So this is an escape pod? What does it actually do?"

"Well, Quizmaster Emma, the luxury escape pod is an extremely high-quality piece of technology, the only desirable way off this ship in its current state…"

"Did he just say what I thought he just said?" Dom asked.

"The luxury escape pod places its users in a trance designed to instigate feelings of happiness and prioritise comfort and safety, while moving at perpetual speed, maximum velocity towards a safe-return location."

"Holy shit, so if the ship itself can't actually return to Earth… are you saying this thing might?" Chloe asked.

"I would not consider that mathematically probable…" Bob said, tempering everyone's expectations. "But it is certainly possible, yes, with the right signcode."

"Oh my god, you guys..." Chloe beamed. "This could be it. Do you hear that, Travis? This could be our ticket out of here!"

Travis didn't make a sound, or if he did, he certainly didn't say anything loud enough to be audible from the other side of the hole in the wall.

"I admire your optimism, Miss Chloe. However, I should just point out that the luxury escape pod has limited capabilities; it will only support up to three individual human beings," Bob said.

"Only three of us? Damn… Two of us are going to have to stay behind?" Dom asked.

"I… I'll s..stay!" Travis called.

"Don't be silly, Travis. We'll… we'll just have to figure this out later. Let's not get ahead of ourselves," Chloe said authoritatively.

"I will be able to unlock the contents of the luxury escape pod very shortly so that we can recover the medicinal cigarette in case of emergency," Bob stated. "Until then, I suggest we return to the common room to complete our quiz."

"Really? I thought we were kind of wrapping up…" Dom said.

"Yet the game is unfinished, Mr. Dom! Mr. Travis has not yet had the opportunity to become quizmaster!"

"Do you honestly think he cares?"

"Come on guys, we might as well get it over with," I said, trying to prevent any of the group's seemingly ageist discrimination from bubbling up again.

We all sat back in the common room, twiddling our thumbs, waiting for Travis to ask a question. For a while, it didn't look like anything was going to come out of his mouth. I looked across at the others: Chloe was tapping her foot impatiently, Emma was trying her hardest not to make eye contact with me, and Dom was fondling his wig and talking to it under his breath as if it were a small puppy, which I found a little disturbing… Travis on the other hand had his eyes shut and was clearly thinking hard – just from a glance at his facial contortions you could tell that there was a lot going on in his weary old brain. At last, he opened his eyes, looked up, and very calmly and clearly asked his question.

"Which one of us is the youngest?" That was not the question I expected him to ask.

"I assume you mean excluding Bob?" Dom asked; Travis nodded.

"Well, wait a second, Bob. Before you go ahead answering this, let's all give this one a shot. Could be interesting…" Chloe said.

"I think Emma's the youngest," I said. That was supposed to be a complement, but Emma made a snorting sound.

"No way!" Chloe yelled. "I'm clearly younger, can't you all tell?"

"Uh… not really," Dom admitted.

"Dominic!"

"Hey, I'm just being honest. You've got a few wrinkles here and there."

"No I haven't. It's the lighting in the room, you know. That and the lack of make up," Chloe sighed.

"Never try to guess a woman's age," I muttered.

"Well, come on, even if what Dom says is true, I still look about 24, 25 perhaps, yeah?" Chloe speculated. "Emma's clearly more in the early to mid thirties."

"Mid thirties?!" Emma snapped.

"Calm down girls, we're actually all in our hundreds or thousands, remember?" I laughed.

"Yeah, well, anyway, come on guys, isn't it obvious I'm the youngest?" Chloe asked.

"I was going to suggest I was the youngest." Dom muttered.

"Dom, no offence. But you're kind of insanely bald. So I doubt it," Chloe scoffed.

"Well, you never know, maybe all my hair fell out when I was like twelve or something…"

"Guys, shall we get this over with?" I asked. "Bob, who's the youngest?"

There was an unexpectedly long pause.

"The youngest is Travis," Bob replied.

Travis stood up.

"Bob's right," he announced.

Then he left the room. Dom, Chloe, Emma and myself all sat in silent shock.

"Oh, yay, another point for me!" Bob cheered.

15

"Now wait a minute…" Chloe paused, about to reveal her seventh theory for why Travis was allegedly the youngest of the group. "I've got it! Travis must have a disease of some sort, like, causing him to age really quickly…"

"That's pretty stupid," Dom said.

"But let's look at the facts," Chloe scratched her head. "We all woke up from cryosleep at the same time, more or less within the same few minutes."

"Yeah, I even saw him as he first climbed out of the pod looking like the grim reaper," Dom reminisced.

"And all the clocks on the pods were set to the same time, so we must have all slept for the same number of years too… So if Travis really is the youngest… Nope, I still don't get it." Chloe said.

"What do you think, Wiggy?" Dom asked.

"Wiggy?" Chloe asked, dumbfounded.

"Yeah," Dom raised his arms, holding his wig in one hand and his artificial beard in the other.

"You…" Chloe raised her eyebrows. "You named your wig…"

"Wiggy." Dom waved with his wig like a pom-pom.

"And the beard?"

"Beardy."

"And you talk to them?" Chloe's voice was getting higher and higher.

"Oh come on, we spend all day talking to an inanimate object already, what's the difference?" Dom lifted Beardy to his ear like a sock puppet and made some exaggerated speaking motions with it. "That's right Beardy, Chloe isn't being very nice to you, is she?"

"But Dom… Dom..." Chloe was trying her hardest not to collapse into laughter. "Dom, Beardy doesn't talk back like Bob does."

"Ohhhh!" Dom gasped. "Chloe, guess what?"

"What?"

"Beardy doesn't like you."

"No, Chloe doesn't," Chloe said. She stepped towards Dom and reached out with her hand, attempting to pull on the edge of the goatee. Dom retaliated with a comical growling sound and continued to animate the puppet hairpiece as if it were attacking her. While it was nice to see Dom coping in his own way with his embarrassing hair loss revelation, this play-fighting was quite excruciating to watch.

Yawn yawn...

Oh, it's my imaginary friend again. Where have you been?

You asked me not to interfere during the quiz, so I obliged.

I suppose you did. But why come back at all? I'd love to say I missed you, X, but, well, I was kinda thinking about what's best for me, actually. You know… the saner, the better?

Do you really believe that there is any sensible definition of sanity under the current circumstances of your space-faring existence?

Well, you're probably right, but I don't think having you around is helping. Come on, why are you bothering me now?

I thought the timing was appropriate.

Why, because Dom's got imaginary friends too now? Is that supposed to make me think talking to you is suddenly justified? Very funny… Well, since you're here, do you fancy shedding any light on the Travis thing?

There's a perfectly rational explanation for everything.

Wait…

"Attack, loyal minions!" Dom had rugby tackled me – I was on the floor near the bookshelves with Wiggy and Beardy playfully tickling my chest. I was having none of it. This wasn't the time for stupid childish wrestling.

"Hey, do you mind? I was in the middle of something," I said angrily, slapping Wiggy out of Dom's grasp.

"What do you mean?" Dom asked.

"I was just…" I paused. "I was just thinking… weren't we supposed to be working out the truth about Travis?"

"Well, yeah, but I don't think we're getting anywhere." Dom said. "Bob's being evasive as ever, and Travis clearly ain't gonna come here and spill the beans himself, so you know what?" Dom lifted up Beardy and ventriloquized the words "Fuck it."

"Come on!" I yelled. "This whole thing makes no sense. All this time Travis hasn't just looked physically older than us, he's acted older than us."

"What are you talking about, I'm mature!" Dom said with surprising conviction, despite lying on top of me like a schoolboy, having just attacked me with a fake beard.

"I mean, it's always been like Travis knows more about the ship than we do. Hell, you saw how he was able to knock up those chairs so quickly. Even if he didn't already look like an old man, he just acts like he's been on this ship for much longer…"

"Despite also being too scared to climb through a little hole in the wall for some reason," Chloe shrugged.

"Don't you guys care? Don't you think it's kinda weird?"

"Kinda weird yes, care no." Dom said with a moronic expression, finally climbing to his feet. "Face it, Joe. Travis is just a weird person, that's all there is to it."

"But…"

"I'm done looking for answers," Dom stifled a yawn, and ran his fingers across his bald scalp. "I know who I am now, Joe. That's all I care about now."

"Oh!" Chloe snapped her fingers and pointed at Wiggy. "Maybe Travis is wearing a wig too! Maybe not just a wig, but like a whole face mask or something, so he's actually got a young looking face underneath. It's not too far-fetched, is it?"

"Uh… What do you want me to do, go over to him and say, 'Sorry Travis, I've just had a sudden urge to tug at your face,' yeah, no, not happening," Dom scoffed.

"Well come on! At least give me one of your theories, if you're gonna keep shooting down mine," Chloe moaned.

"Okay, fine. He's a cyborg that runs on purple juice," Dom guessed.

"Rubbish."

"How about… maybe everyone on this ship just started aging backwards? So we all start out looking old, finish up looking young?"

"Are you implying I'm the oldest now?" Chloe frowned.

Before Dom could either take back his theory or follow it up with a witty remark, Emma burst into the room. She'd been in the airlock room with Bob all this time.

"Guys, you might want to see this," she called.

The luxury escape pod was there in front of us, opening up like an egg to reveal three perfectly contoured silver seats made of a soft plush material undoubtedly a thousand times cosier than the Travis-chairs or even our lost, fabled sofa. Above them, loads of glowing cables and important-looking pieces of futuristic technology were strewn around, making for quite the spectacle.

"As I stated previously, the luxury escape pod places its users in a trance designed to instigate feelings of happiness and prioritise comfort and safety," Bob stated. "I managed to disengage the activation locks and initiate the authentication matrix. It is ready for use as soon as you are ready."

"Amazing… We might actually be able to get out of here," Dom muttered, seemingly forgetting about the rather substantial issue of there only being room for three of us in there.

"What about the cigarette cure thing? Did you find it?" Chloe asked.

"Negative," Bob replied. "This is most curious. It appears to have been removed from its storage container."

"All we found is this," Emma said, holding a shiny red lighter in her palm. She flicked a switch and a tiny flame emerged, in case any of us had, post-memory-loss, struggled to remember what a lighter was supposed to do.

"Well it's no use without the ciggy itself, is it?" Chloe asked. "Did you check everywhere?"

"Affirmative, Miss Chloe."

"I've been looking all over the ship for it," Emma added.

"Well, hopefully we'll never need it," I said. "We'll be fine without it, surely?"

"What makes you so sure?" Chloe asked.

"Well, I mean, let's just get our priorities straight. How the heck do we decide who gets to go in the pod and who gets to stay behind?" I tapped my foot impatiently.

"I don't know, Joe." Chloe said, flustered. "I just don't know. Now's not the right time…"

"Well when is the right time? When will ever be the right time?" I was starting to feel my blood boiling.

"Joe…"

"Next time you and Dom are playing the Muppet Beard Show, is that when it'll be the right time?"

"Calm down, Joe," Emma sighed.

"Alright guys, let's split up and look for that cigarette," Chloe said, looking away.

"Chloe, we don't need it!" I shouted. "I… I don't need it. I don't want it. I'm not sick… I'm not…" I trailed off, realising I was only digging myself a bigger hole. Chloe stared at me in disgust then strode off with Emma and Dom.

"I'll just close this up for now then," Bob said as the luxury escape pod closed back to its original solid, round state. I figured it would be a while before we'd be able to properly discuss who should go and who should say, and that I probably shouldn't risk aggravating anyone further in the meantime…

Still, I refused to accept the notion that I was sick. Those things I'd been imagining? Bob's elevator music? My imaginary friend? What did it really matter? I'm only as sane as everyone else, I told myself. X was right, there was no sensible definition of sanity out here. Either we were all sick, or none of us were. Though if there was one thing I had to believe in… I was about to reach into my pocket when Bob called across to me.

"By the way, Mr. Joe, I have another communications transcript for you!"

"What?"

"Here you go!"

// 921372 Decryptions in Progress…
**_Run{BrdCms_PK01} AND DeductPrevRenderState 05320
_Disp{BrdCms_PK01}
// Rendering**

// Broadcast Communications Transcript 212.1.D7

AS >> Yo.

CO << Copy that. Who is this?

AS >> Come on, you know who it is. Senior technician on board the Atom Sierra.

CO << Look, we've been through this before. Please use the standard greetings terminology when…

AS >> Yeah I know, sorry. I can never remember that damn signcode. It isn't stored on any of our drives either. You know what security's like.

CO << Well, you must have it written down somewhere, surely?

AS >> Yeah of course. But you should see my desk, bloody hell. Samples all over the place. It's probably here somewhere. Do you want me to look? Might take a while, I'll have to sort through all these books.

CO << Just make sure you have it to hand next time.

AS >> I will, I promise. Just gotta tidy up, I swear.

CO << Don't say that like it's not your fault. Why do you have so many books lying around? I mean, who the hell reads books these days?

AS >> You'd be surprised.

CO << Well, whatever. Your advisor's here now, I'm patching you through.

< HOLD >

CO << You have no idea how pissed my boss is at you right now.

AS >> Meh, what's he gonna do, cut my salary?

CO << No, that's not the issue, it's just that… if anything happens, anything goes wrong, you know we won't be able to contact you.

AS >> Come on… It's a straightforward analysis mission, what could possibly go wrong?

CO << Well, what's the latest on the Simmons / Hammond situation?

AS >> Oh dear, don't get me started on that…

CO << Is it true?

AS >> Yeah, she's pregnant. How about that, eh? Knew I was onto something.

CO << That… must be awkward.

AS >> Tell me about it. And we're stuck out here with no bloody contraception on board. Bit of an oversight there…

CO << So much for the professional code of conduct.

145

AS >> Yeah, well, tell that to the idiot who thinks it's fair to recruit hot young mixed gender teams to spend months of their lives in a few square meters of living space. It's a freaking love nest in here.

CO << This is why we have the sterilization services. Guess with this industry they'll have to be stricter in the future.

AS >> Yeah, more to the point we've got a god damn space baby on the way.

CO << She could still have an abortion, surely? The bots must know what to do.

AS >> Yeah, I honestly don't think she's going to go through with that. She's thinking of keeping the child.

CO << Jesus. If this gets out we'll have another damn scandal on our hands. Another one for the headlines…

AS >> Yeah, and it's thrown our cryosleep plans into jeopardy too. The long freezing process ain't good for pregnancies, apparently.

CO << Not considering the timescales you'd be keeping to…

AS >> Yeah, it'd be good if you could just thaw out a frozen pod at any old time but that just ain't how it works. Gotta be committed to the long nap. Don't think any of us are now. I guess we'll just have to sit it out.

CO << Dammit, that's a big chunk of mission data we'd all be missing out on. Don't think the seniors are going to be happy with that.

AS >> Oh come on, since when have we ever been able to meet all the deliverables?

CO << Indeed. So anyway, your wife is here. Thought you might like to have a catch-up.

AS >> Yes please!

CO << Be careful. You know the drill, saying your family members' names on here is strictly prohibited. Security's clamping down on these things.

AS >> Come on, man. Nobody's listening.

CO << It's the transcripts we're worried about. Can't wipe 'em any more. Hell, nobody knows where or when people could be reading this stuff.

AS >> Jeez, maybe I shouldn't have kept going on about zero-G intercourse that other time…

CO << Well, quite. Anyway, I'm putting you through now.

< HOLD >

CO << Hi darling!

AS >> Hi… Hello…

CO << What is it?

AS >> Nothing, just… It feels like such a long time since we've spoken. I don't really know what to say.

CO << It's weird isn't it. So how have you been?

AS >> Surviving, you know me. We've been getting a lot of samples recently. It's kind of dull though. Space isn't all it's cracked up to be.

CO << It's been a long month…

AS >> Oh man, how are we gonna last the whole next three years?

CO << We knew what you were signing up for. It'll be okay, sweetie.

AS >> Yeah…

CO << By the way, there's someone special here for you.

AS >> Oh my…

CO << Daddy?

AS >> Hey, hey, how have you been, little man?

CO << Daddy! Look what I made!

AS >> Is that… Is that a little space ship you've got there?

CO << Yes yes and it's all mine! Woosh! Nyeeooo! <unintelligible sounds>

AS >> Aw, that's cute, son. Man, I wish I was allowed to say your name on here.

CO << Look how fast it can go, Daddy!

AS >> Yeah, that's really great, I… actually, I'm not sure you should be playing with that indoors, what does Mummy say?

CO << Mummy says I should be responsi… responsible for my actions.

AS >> Yeah, well, I'm not sure you want to be responsible for burning down the whole of Central Office. Be careful!

CO << When I grow up I wanna be a spaceman just like you, Daddy!

AS >> That's wonderful son, now can you put that down? Look, Mummy wants you to put it down now.

CO << But Daddy, I…

AS >> Listen to your mother, son.

CO << Aw… Do I have to…

AS >> Yes.

CO << Oh…kay… Daddy… When are you going to come home?

AS >> Daddy's on a very important mission, son. It's going to take some time.

CO << Are you going to be here for Christmas Daddy?

AS >> Son, I…

CO << I miss you, Daddy.

AS >> I miss you too…

CO << Daddy, what does this button do?

AS >> Um, no, don't press that. It ends the broadcast… oh, you're pressing it aren't you. Well, so much for logistics…

< Unexpected Transcript File Reset to {BrdCms_PK02} >
_Run{BrdCms_PK02} // Error 05377 – Task Not Yet Started
_ContinueTasks

"I still don't know what you're on about, Bob," I said as I climbed through the hole back to the corridor. "I don't see any transcripts or anything, but, uh... thanks?"

"No problem, Mr. Joe!" Bob called. "Would you mind giving me a lift to the common room?"

I froze mid-step and did an awkward roll back into the airlock room.

"Yeah, sure, whatever..." I grumpily trudged back to the luxury escape pod and placed Bob into my pocket.

After dropping Bob off in the common room and stumbling past Dom, Chloe and Emma, who were sorting through the cables in the corridor, I turned towards the bathroom.

"You'll have to wait, Travis is in there," Dom called out, but I tried the door anyway. To my surprise, it wasn't locked.

I found Travis standing facing the sink with his back to me. Not wanting to be awkward, I said hello. At first there was no response.

"I know what you're after," Travis said, softly. I was taken aback.

"What do you mean? The cigarette?" I asked. "The others are looking for it, but..."

"But you don't want it," Travis said. He turned around slowly. In his hand... there it was. The single, inconspicuous looking cigarette, already lit.

"What... what have you done?" I stammered. I almost dropped to the floor in shock. Travis had stolen the so-called cure – was he trying to waste it?

"You'll never accept the prognosis," Travis inhaled a puff of smoke and breathed it out directly into my face. The fumes rose up into the ceiling and quickly escaped through some kind of vent, leaving no actual trace behind. "That's the problem. You'll never accept that you're the sick one."

I was speechless. Right now it definitely didn't look like I was the one we should be worrying about. I'd never heard

Travis speak so clearly. His stammer had completely disappeared.

"Don't worry. This is just regular tobacco." Travis rubbed the butt of the cigarette on the edge of the sink. "The cure's still intact. At the end of the cigarette, you see?"

I nervously stepped forward. There was a faint ring around the opposite end of the cigarette showing that something else was inside it.

"Leading with the tobacco, it's an interesting move. Get you addicted before they get you cured. I guess the medical industry must have its pockets in the tobacco business as well. Everyone has to make a living."

"I don't understand, Travis."

"Sorry, I'm rambling. Still getting used to talking this much. This shit is really loosening me up. Where was I?"

"The cigarette…" I pointed, trembling, and still finding it incredibly hard to adjust to the new Travis, high and talkative.

"Right, yeah, they must've designed it like this so people like you'd smoke it all before they even knew what was in it. That's the idea, trick people into curing themselves of their mental ailments. The people they designed this for never believe there's anything wrong with them, never willingly accept a cure. A little detail Bob seems to have neglected."

"Wha…" I gasped.

"But, since the cat's already out of the bag… I knew I'd have to get the cure ready for you… make it as simple as possible when the moment comes. Even if that means distributing it via some other means. The water supply, the air vents…" I watched again as the smoke dissipated through the ceiling, and covered my mouth.

"It's okay. Like I said, I haven't reached the cure yet. There's a load left to smoke through first. You're breathing regular old tobacco…" Travis paused for a brief coughing fit. "Advanced technology, this cigarette. It can be lit and relit again and again," Travis tapped the edge of the cigarette against a familiar bright red object.

"Travis… What the hell are you talking about? Where did you get…"

"This lighter?" It was exactly the same lighter as before. "I borrowed it from Emma."

"No, the cigarette! Where did you get the cigarette?" I asked, desperately.

"You want to know where I found it?" Travis laughed. "They stuck it in the fridge. It was glued to back of the inside wall, you'd never have known…"

"The fridge?" I was stunned. "Wait… So back when we first went to the kitchen and you were looking inside the fridge… you were actually getting the cigarette out? You've known about it all this time?"

Travis sighed and nodded. "After the incident, when the panel to the escape pod area was sealed off, they knew they'd have to move the cigarette. Somewhere closer, so that it would be within reach if another crisis came around. They weren't betting on everyone losing their memories, though. I guess that's what a really, really long sleep will do to you…"

"Who's they? How do you know all this?" I growled.

"I'm not like you guys." Travis said. "I remember. I remember everything."

I grabbed Travis by the neck and pushed him to the wall, restraining him with my elbow.

"Tell me!" I raged. "Who are you?!"

"You really want to know who I am, or should I just cure you now?" Travis choked, making like he was about to shove the cigarette down my throat. Panting, I relaxed my grip and wiped the sweat from my brow.

"I was conceived and born on this ship." Travis coughed. "It was an accident. I was the child that wasn't supposed to be."

I stared, open-mouthed, perplexed, slowly stepping back. What the hell was he implying?

"Don't act like you don't know," Travis continued. "I know Bob's been sending you transcripts."

"That's what he told me, but I swear I haven't seen them!" I cried. "I don't know where to look!"

"Hm…" Travis sounded saddened. "It might already be too late…"

"What are you talking about? Born on this ship? I don't understand."

"Yes, I was born here. My parents… my parents are…"

"No…" I said, trembling. "Don't say it."

"It doesn't even matter now," Travis lamented. He paused and turned towards me with a piercing gaze. "The only person that matters is you."

"I don't get it," My head was spinning. "What did I do?"

"You sabotaged the whole mission, Joe." Travis' words were like a knife. "It was all because of you… I had to stop you. But I was young, weak, just a boy… all I could do was freeze you with the others." The aggression in Travis' words was echoed in his body language – now thoroughly intimidating.

"But you…" I gasped in disbelief. "We were all frozen together, even you…" I gasped.

"No. I couldn't join you at first. The pods don't work on children…" Travis turned away, breathing slowly. "I waited… I grew up… found out about the cure… I tried to find a way to unfreeze you to give you the cure but the dials can't be altered on the pods already in use…" Travis paused to have a coughing fit. "One day after I'd waited long enough, I tried to catch up."

"Catch up?"

"Yes, by freezing myself too. I was old enough at that point. I set the dial on the remaining pod so that I'd wake up at the same time…"

"But the dials on the pods said you slept the same length of time as everyone else. You must have started at the same time too!" I insisted.

"You're forgetting what Bob told us before." Travis smiled, weakly. "The dials on the pods. Rolling over every 256 years. I didn't understand that at first. I changed the dial so that the number matched the others, thinking I'd catch up with the rest of you, but I didn't, I was years off. It was trial and error, every single time. I'd wake and it would be weeks before my pod would recharge and I could try again. I did this so many times, I began to grow frail…"

I slumped against the wall, desperately trying to take this all in.

"The final time the dials rolled over, I had the timing figured out. The last 25 years. Perfectly synced at last…" Travis coughed once again.

"So because you had shorter sleeps… you never lost your memories?" I asked, my voice starting to break.

"Not to the extent of the others," Travis said. "I knew the cigarette was important, couldn't remember why. It all came back to me during the quiz."

"Travis…" I finally whispered. "Whatever it is that I did… I don't even want to know, but that's not me any more. I promise…"

Travis turned back to the sink.

"Prove it. Take the cigarette," Travis said, holding the so-called cure out in front of him. "Please. All you've got to do is smoke the rest and you'll be cured. It's the only way I can be sure."

I froze. What was I supposed to do? Someone was knocking on the bathroom door. I shuffled backwards, eyes still fixated on Travis and nervously felt for the door latch, sliding it across to make sure it was locked.

"Joe? Travis? Who's in there?" It was Dom.

"Take it!" Travis waved the cigarette right at me. The knocking grew louder. I closed my eyes. My head was throbbing harder than it ever had before.

"Please…" Travis' chin wobbled with desperation. "Before it's too late…"

"I don't smoke." I didn't know whether I was lying.

KNOCK KNOCK KNOCK KNOCK.

"Okay." I said, taking the lighter and the now-cool cigarette from Travis' hands. "I'll think about it."

"If you don't go through with it," Travis said calmly. "When the moment comes, she'll be ready."

Do you really believe that there is any sensible definition of sanity under the current circumstances of your space-faring existence?

I'm only as sane as everyone else.

16

The bathroom door swung open. Apparently I hadn't locked the door at all; that or the latch had stopped working. Dom stood in the doorway with a bizarre expression that seemed to transition through a whole range of different feelings in about one second. His embarrassment at having intruded on our privacy quickly gave way to confusion as to why both me and Travis were in there.

"Oh, I'm… sorry?" Dom's intonation went up an octave. Me and Travis blinked.

"I just really needed to… Shit! Why do you have that?" Dom pointed right at me. For a horrible moment I thought he'd spotted the cigarette, but then I realised that I'd already instinctively dabbed it out and stuffed it into my pocket - it was the lighter Dom had noticed. I was still holding it out at arm's length. My stomach dropped as I realised what Dom thought I was doing.

"Joe. Get away from Travis, now." Dom said, seriously.

"This isn't what it looks like, Dom," I breathed.

"Drop the lighter!" Dom yelled.

"I wasn't…"

"Drop it!"

I raised both of my arms in surrender and the lighter fell to the floor with a clank. Nothing I could have said would have made any difference at this point. Travis had gone silent again, the two-faced…

"For god's sake, Joe," Dom picked up the lighter and pulled me out into the hallway. "We can't leave you out of our sight for more than a few minutes can we…" I stared at the ground despondently.

"Look," Dom paused as if he were about to reason with me. "I know you want to know the truth about Travis, Joe. But threatening him isn't the solution, okay, it just isn't." I didn't have the strength to admit to Dom that Travis had just willingly told me the truth about himself anyway.

Emma came over.

"What's going on here?" she asked.

"Joe was threatening Travis with this," Dom replied, rattling the lighter about in his hand.

"What the hell?"

"We can't let him walk around like this any more," Dom sighed.

"He's gonna get someone hurt," Emma said. As if I wasn't standing there listening to every word the two of them were saying.

"I'm sorry Joe, I'm gonna… I'm gonna have to restrain you," Dom dropped the lighter again, grabbed my arms forcefully and started to drag me down the corridor. I didn't know what he was planning to do, tie me to a pipe or something, but he didn't get very far.

"Wait!" Travis called. He stepped out of the bathroom. "Let him go. It's okay."

Dom looked dumbfounded. "No, Travis. It's not okay. You could have gotten hurt or -"

"He wasn't threatening me," Travis replied. "I gave him the lighter. I was showing him how it worked, that's all."

"Really?"

"Yes, Dom. Let him go." Travis had conviction in his eyes.

Dom frustratedly turned from Travis, to Emma, to me. "Well, why didn't you say anything, Joe?" he growled.

"I tried…" I said, softly.

"Hardly," Dom scoffed.

"Because I knew you'd never believe me," I replied. Dom sighed loudly and finally let go of me. He stood up, seemingly remembering what his business was a few moments ago and heading towards the bathroom.

"Excuse me," he said, awkwardly brushing past Travis. The door closed and I heard the latch slide across, which as established meant the door probably wasn't actually locked.

"I think we should try fixing that lock," I said, trying to break the ice. "I mean, we could always, just, like… get one of those metal poles from the corridor and jam that behind the door, that'd work as a lock, right?"

Travis walked away.

"Well, never mind, just an idea, that's all…" I mumbled.

Emma reached out with her hand. For a moment I thought she was offering to pull me up from the ground, so I reached out as well. Instead, she picked up the lighter. I should have known better by this point.

"I'll take this, thank you very much," she said. I sat there for a few moments, hand outstretched, a thousand swear words at the tip of my tongue. My hand became a clenched fist, and the swear words fizzled out into a pathetic frustrated groan. Nope, keep it cool… I stood up despondently.

Chloe was lying down in the common room. She'd amusingly got three of the Travis-chairs lined up so that they essentially resembled a wonkier version of the sofa, and had decided to lay across them face-down for a bit of shut-eye.

"Comfy?" I asked, sarcastically.

"No."

She seemed exhausted. I think she'd been looking for the cigarette for the past few hours. A few seconds later she tried to roll over but ended up kicking over one of the chairs in the process and almost hitting her head on the ground.

"I'm fine," she said, body half-dangling from another chair that had just fallen sideways.

"Are you?"

"Just gimme a sec." She shuffled around for the next 30 seconds trying to sit upright, finally managing it after untangling her leg and sending another chair flying across the room. She sighed.

"What is it, Joe?"

"Nothing, I…" I felt the cigarette in my pocket and caught Travis' eye from across the room. "I just want to apologise for earlier, for acting like I don't need that cure, I mean…"

"What was that stuff that happened with Dom just now?" Chloe asked.

"Oh that… that was just a misunderstanding," I said, downplaying things.

"A misunderstanding, huh," Chloe yawned.

"I wish it wasn't like this," I vented. "It feels like everything I do is misunderstood, like I'm always one step away from you guys turning completely against me, abandoning me."

"It doesn't have to be like that, Joe." Chloe said.

"Yes, it does," I replied. "There's only three spaces available on that escape pod thing, I get it."

"Get what?"

"You guys need scapegoats. You need people to stay behind. I guess I've gone and volunteered myself again. I get it."

"It doesn't have to be like that…"

"Why?"

"Because we care about you, Joe." Chloe's voice quavered. "We do… We all do, even Dom, though he doesn't like to admit it. Why do you think we're so bothered about finding that cure for you?"

I was silent. The cure… The cure that was in my pocket right now. All I had to do was find out where Emma had taken the lighter…

Chloe kept talking. "You keep scaring us, you know that. But… you did save us, after all. You found those backups and if it wasn't for you, we wouldn't even know about the escape pod."

"Thank you." I said.

"No, Joe. Thank *you*."

I walked over to Chloe and gave her a hug. Finally I felt some kind of friendly warmth from someone. It wasn't much, but to me it meant the world. Perhaps I still had the time to redeem myself.

As everyone retreated to their bedrooms, I found it difficult to get to sleep. There was too much going on in my mind. Those revelations Travis had given me all added up but it was difficult to accept that… that man could be my son. Or Dom's. Chloe or Emma… one of them was the mother. These people who were still strangers to me in the present had enjoyed a whole other life together in the past, a life I had been a part of and was apparently somehow responsible for ending. And now what was happening? I was becoming dangerous again? Was history going to repeat itself as Travis had suggested?

I had the cigarette… All I had to do was get the lighter from Emma and I'd be able to give them all the peace of mind that yes, I was fine. I would no longer be walking on eggshells. I would have the chance to get out of this mental prison.

What was the problem? I looked out of the window from the common room. I couldn't see the asteroid. Real or not, I knew I'd have to keep it to myself. I would just have to pretend it wasn't there. I would be the Joe they all wanted me to be. Not the rambling lunatic I'd been portrayed as. Yes. Fuck you, asteroid. Fuck you, X.

"Oh, hello, Mr. Joe." Bob had decided to slowly and with great indignity hop his way into my room.

"Go away, Bob. I'm asleep." I said.

"I detect that is probably a lie, Mr. Joe." Bob declared.

"What do you want?"

"Another transcript for you!"

"Another one?"

"Correct! I will send it to you as you requested. Good night!"

"You know I can't read them, but whatever, Bob. Good night."

// 842195 Decryptions in Progress…
_Run{BrdCms_PK02}
for Lines=1 to (X)
MergeState_2122(70)4// DedupeUnwantedLines
_Disp{BrdCms_PK02}
// Rendering

// Broadcast Communications Transcript 212.2.F4

AS >> Hello?

CO <<

AS >> Uh, are you there, central?

CO <<

AS >> I just want someone to talk to...

CO << (Unintelligible)

AS >> Sorry?

CO << (Unintelligible) got to get (Unintelligible) sign… code.

AS >> Ah, jeez, you're breaking up. Hang on, a minute, the damn baby's crawling around on the transmitter again, just a sec.

CO << (Unintelligible)

AS >> Sorry about that, what were you saying?

CO << The signcode, come on…

AS >> Oh yeah, about that…

CO << Don't tell me you lost it again.

AS >> I lost it again.

CO << Why am I not surprised? Look, it's not just a formality thing, you know. That code contains the exact coordinates of Earth. It's not something you want to leave lying around.

AS >> Okay but it legitimately isn't my fault this time. Do you know what it's like having a baby on board a spaceship?

160

CO << No, I don't. Because it's illegal.

AS >> And now I know why. I swear, it can't be good for the poor tyke. I wouldn't be surprised if he grows up to be a right little psychopath.

CO << Hey, that's a little harsh, don't you think?

AS >> Yeah, I'm sorry, it's just… you have no idea how frustrating it is up here. We're having to fashion nappies out of toilet rolls and towels. I'm on clean-up duties. Sometimes wish I could just jettison the makeshift nappies out the airlock, it just ain't hygienic having to clean 'em and reuse 'em all the time.

CO << Ew… On the bright side hopefully you'll wind up teaching him how to make, uh, economical use of resources. Alright… How are things, otherwise?

AS >> Other than being woken up by endless wailing and having to crawl around on my hands and feet all day long trying to keep the kid entertained and out of danger? What do you mean, otherwise?

CO << Aren't the parents taking care of all that?

AS >> 'The parents.' Ha. No naming and shaming on here…

CO << Well, aren't they?

AS >> Of course they are, but I mean, there's no escaping baby-land. Think of the square meterage we've got. You can do a lap of the whole ship in about 30 seconds.

CO << Yeah, I'm sorry about that. I did try to push for the larger living quarters. Still, how exactly do you keep the kid out of danger? Not exactly a kid-friendly place is it – even with the retro design?

AS >> Keeping him out of the airlock control room is the main priority, I think. We can't have the silly kid climbing into the decompression chamber and blasting off all by himself.

CO << Isn't there a plan to make sure that doesn't happen? I mean he was crawling all over your transmitter a minute ago…

AS >> Well, don't worry, we'll make damn sure he doesn't ever climb through to the airlock room in the first place. The access hatch is half-way up the wall so he can't reach it. Just have to whip out the old pyscho-disciplinary doodads for when he gets taller, I'm sure we'll manage.

CO << I'm sorry. How long has it been?

AS >> Since the birth? Oh, I dunno, jeez, probably about 3 months. Just over a year since we first set off, and my god am I bored of space.

CO << You'll stick it out, I know you will.

AS >> Haven't really got much of a choice, have I. Just wish I could see my wife and son again, frankly, are they there right now?

CO << No, I'm sorry. We haven't been able to authorize any more family meetings.

AS >> Why not?

CO << My boss thinks you're a lost cause. That talk of a rescue team has subsided, I'm afraid you're gonna have to come back the long way.

AS >> Swinging back around Saturn? Jeez, with the burnout we've suffered that's gonna take at least, what, three, four years? I'd rather take the ole' luxo-exo for a spin.

CO << Yeah, don't think things are quite that desperate yet, plus the mission isn't even complete. You know the protocol right?

AS >> Not that desperate? Are you having a laugh? We could have died a couple weeks back!

CO << What do you mean?

AS >> You didn't get the memo? Had a close call from a rogue Kuiper object.

CO << Oh?

AS >> Yeah, it's true. Giant-ass rock, came outta nowhere, scraped the edge of the ship, almost took out the kitchen in the process.

CO << Wow, an asteroid? I had no idea. On the bright side, at least you're still all here.

AS >> Kinda wish it had been a bit more dramatic, to be honest. The first collision a ship has had with an extraterrestrial object in decades and I totally slept through it.

CO << Have you had a chance to assess the damage?

AS >> Oh, the ship is fine, obviously. All systems seem to be green, I doubt any foreign particles got lodged anywhere, so we're all good.

CO << Well I should hope so, especially with a newborn on board.

AS >> Yeah, definitely. Um… Oh dear, sorry, I'm gonna have to go. The little bugger is trying to swallow up the intelbot.

CO << Uh-oh! Choking hazard!

AS >> Tell me about it. That's the fifth time this has happened. Hey, put it down! Bad baby!

CO << Well, now you've just made him cry. Any other tricks up your sleeve?

AS >> No, I think I'll leave that to the parents. I'm tired, I think I'm gonna go grab a coffee and call it a day.

CO << Right-o. Take care.

< Central office signing out >
// End Transcript

17

The following morning, instead of getting up, I laid in my room for a few hours, listening to the whirring sounds of the ship, focusing on every little detail. I was tired, but today was going to be the day, I decided. I was going to take control, I wasn't going to talk to X any more. I would be in control of my senses.

Emma and Bob were talking. I closed my eyes and focused on the conversation.

"And what about you, Bob? What will you do when we go off in the escape pod?" Emma asked.

"Oh, I will stay here, of course," Bob said, excitedly.

"Stay? But there's bound to be room for you in the pod with us. You're tiny." Emma said.

"Why would I want to go with you, Miss Emma?" Bob asked.

"You could go back to Earth, back where you were made. Wouldn't that be what you want?"

"To live in a technological museum or to be dissected by the descendants of my creators?" Bob mused. "I think not, Miss Emma. Staying here would be much more exciting."

"I'm not sure exciting is the right word, Bob…"

"On the contrary! I find it tremendously exciting to be in such a deeply uncharted region of the universe. It is all I could ever ask for…"

"Why? What will you do, exactly?"

"I will wait," Bob declared. "I will continue to wait as the ship continues on its linear trajectory into the unknown. I am most lucky that the resources utilised on this ship and in my very construction are self-renewing by design."

"Won't that get boring?"

"I do not find perpetual existence boring, Miss Emma. One day I may stumble upon an advanced alien civilisation and discover fascinating truths about the universe!"

"I thought you said there was virtually no chance of that happening…"

"For a mortal being, perhaps…" Bob paused. "However, by the sheer definition of my functionally infinite lifespan, it is likely that in the next few trillion years I myself will experience many of the hypothetical wonders of the universe!"

"Like what?"

"The Big Crunch."

"What's that?"

"One of the theorized scenarios for the end of the universe involving the ultimate singular collapse of the entirety of space and everything in it."

"Sounds like fun."

"I know, right?"

"You really think you'd last long enough to see that, Bob?"

"Well, one would hope so. I suppose that plan could always fail in the meantime if the ship came into contact with a rogue object like an asteroid or…"

I'd heard enough. The mere mention of the word 'asteroid' was enough to make me sit bolt upright and walk away. The last thing I needed was something to remind me of that…

I stumbled across to the kitchen and sat down. It was too early for breakfast - the purple flakes weren't ready yet, but I sat down anyway. I rubbed my forehead slowly and looked around. There wasn't much here, but the kitchen knife was resting ominously on the table. I picked it up and examined the blade carefully. It was sharp, certainly something that could be brandished as a weapon and definitely not the sort of object I could imagine the others would have wanted me near. But screw that! I jabbed the knife into the table. This was the day that I was going to make a point, to prove that I wasn't dangerous. I just had to get the lighter from Emma and figure out when the best time was to smoke that cure…

I continued to play around with the knife. Before long I somehow found myself placing my left hand on the table and started playing the five-finger knife game, stabbing the knife into the gaps between my fingers. It was surprisingly easy, I thought. I was doing it pretty slowly to be fair, yet the adrenaline rush was still there.

This was brilliant. I increased my speed, stabbing between my fingers, feeling the tiny draught of air each time I raised the knife before jamming it down millimetres away from my flesh. I didn't know why I was doing this, but it felt good. Stab. Stab. Stab. Stab. Stab. Back and forth. Faster and faster. I was in control of my senses. It was all going to…

"Gah!" I hissed softly. The knife went through my index finger, straight to the bone. The pain was intense and… and… wait. No it wasn't. There was no blood, it was as if the knife had gone straight through to the table, as if my hand were a hologram or…

The breakfast bell chimed; I looked up as Emma, Chloe and Dom came groggily trudging in. I looked again at my hand. The knife had vanished. I had never even been holding it. I looked to where the knife had originally been, lying flat on the table. It was still there. It had never moved an inch. I…

"Morning Joe," Dom yawned.

"Morning," I said, massaging my index finger which, of course, had no injury. I watched silently as breakfast was served, sitting in contemplation as the others ate their way through depressing purple sludge.

"Aren't you gonna have yours, Joe?" Chloe asked. "Are you feeling okay?"

I paused.

"No, Chloe. No I'm not." I spoke softly, reaching into my pocket. Travis' eyes widened, he got up and walked out, presumably to get the lighter. He probably thought there was no use holding out any longer, we were going to have to fix this right here, right now, before I felt any worse…

"There's something I have to tell you guys…" I began. I was on the cusp of telling Dom, Chloe and Emma about the cigarette cure that I'd kept in my pocket all this time, but then my eye caught something across the room. It was something I'd been neglecting for a while now. I'd been trying not to think about it, but there it was. The coffee machine.

Wait…

"Where is it?" I asked. I was searching deep into both of my pockets, becoming frantic. It wasn't the cigarette I was after now.

"What are you looking for?" Dom asked.

"I'm sure it was right here…" I said.

"Joe!" Dom snapped.

I took a deep breath.

"The coffee sachet. From my pocket. Emma, where is it?"

"I don't know what you did with it, Joe…" Emma sighed.

"No, no, no… One of you has it. I couldn't just lose something like that!" I snarled.

"I don't have a clue what you're talking about Joe! Don't do this, you're scaring me," Chloe whimpered.

"No, this is important!" I banged my fists on the table. "One of you has been through my pockets, I need that sachet!"

"We haven't been in your pockets!" Dom yelled.

I stood up quickly.

"Maybe you haven't," I said softly. "But I know who has."

I darted to the door with a flash, slamming it shut behind me.

"Joe, stop!" Emma cried. No, nobody was going to stop me getting that sachet back. Remembering my earlier idea about securely locking doors, I grabbed a pole from the corridor walls and jammed it behind the kitchen door just as

Dom was about to open it. He hammered on it with all his might and yelled out.

"Joe! Open the door!" But it was to no avail; the pole had jammed it shut. Dom, Chloe and Emma were all trapped in the kitchen.

"I have to do this!" I yelled from the other side.

"JOOOOOOEEEEE!!!!"

I stormed into the common room. Bob was on the table.

"Oh, hello there, Mr. Joe. I have another transcript for y…"

"WHERE'S MY DAMN COFFEE?!" I yelled.

"I beg your pardon? Perhaps the new transcript can wait for…"

I grabbed Bob and threw him forcefully across the room. He hit the wall hard and bounced across the floor, letting out a very convincing scream.

"You know what I'm talking about!" I yelled. "It was in my pocket!"

"What are you talking about Mr. – waaaah!" Bob screamed as I picked him up and threw him over to the other side of the room.

"I know it was you! You were in my pocket, Bob! You remember? When you asked me for that 'lift' back from the escape pod room. That's… that's when you must have taken it!"

"Mr. Joe, I did not… You see, I do not have any hands…"

I grabbed Bob again and squeezed him against my thumb.

"And just what were you doing in my room last night?"

"I… was delivering another transcript..."

"Imaginary transcripts I can't see or hear, huh, yeah, nothing dodgy about that at all… totally not scrambling my brain, making me crazy…" I squeezed tighter.

"Please re…refrain from doing this," Bob stammered.

"For Christ's sake, you… You were INSIDE my body at one point, Bob. What have you been doing to me all this time?!"

"I was saving your life after you almost died from Operation Sofa Space, Mr. Joe. Don't you remember?"

"All your faffing around before and during the quiz… That music I heard… I was the only one who heard it. You played it just for me, didn't you! Just to make me freak out…"

"Mr. Joe…"

"The asteroid! You know about the asteroid don't you? You even mentioned it this morning. The asteroid out there!" I pointed out of the window at the glowing white mass.

"There is an asteroid?" Bob asked with naïve curiosity.

"Yes, Bob! Don't deny it! You namedropped it when I was listening to you and Emma because you knew, you fucking knew it would set me off didn't you…"

"Where is this asteroid, Mr. Joe? I cannot see it. Perhaps you would like to help me look for it?"

"No, no…" I dropped Bob on the floor and closed my eyes. "I'm not playing any fucking games with you, Bob. I've had enough of those from X…"

"X? What is X?"

I laughed maniacally. "X is my imaginary friend. He's been talking to me, you know. Trying to make me question what's real. You've been doing the exact same thing!"

"Mr. Joe, I must confess, I am at a real loss here. Perhaps I can calm you down with a joke or two?"

"A joke?"

"Knock knock…"

"It's you!" I yelled. My mouth widened. "You're X, aren't you, Bob? It's… you!"

"Mr. Joe?"

"DON'T YOU 'MR. JOE' ME!" I yelled, kicking Bob into the side of the table. "You've been in my head all this time, haven't you?!"

"M…Mister…J…Joe…"

"I've finally figured it out," I mumbled. "I didn't screw up the mission all those years ago. I saved us. From you!" I gasped.

"I do not follow."

"Oh, don't start with the whole 'do not follow' routine, you useless metal slab," I ranted. "That whole conversation with Emma this morning, about what you really want? To keep this ship going in the same fucking direction for ever and ever until you find out what's at the end of the universe or some shit? The little robot who wanted to see it all… pitting us feeble humans against each other to get his wish!"

"You've… got… it… wrong…"

"Well I'm through with all of this!" I raised my foot above Bob's tiny, helpless body, ready to stomp him into oblivion. "One last chance, Bob…"

"Please…"

"Shut up and tell me where the coffee is."

"Not possible…"

"What?"

"Cannot shut up and answer your question at the same time. Not possible… Can't do it… Can't…"

"Oh, what's the matter? Can't handle the logical contradictions again? Aw… too bad." I smirked. "Come on… Where is the coffee?!"

"I don't know!"

"I know you know…"

"I don't! How can you know I know when I know I don't know? Do not understand… Too many contradictions…"

"Well let's try this… Hey Bob, you're the cleverest on the ship."

"Why thank you?!" Bob seemed confused.

"But I'm still cleverer than you," I smirked.

"But you just said I was the… ohhhh… no… can't handle… Do not want…" Sparks were starting to form around the edge of Bob's exterior.

"Oh, boo hoo. Did your successful plan just fail?"

"But… how can a plan be a success and a failure at the same time? Uhh… Must stop… Must shut down… Must shut down…"

"Hey, Bob. I'm so sorry that I'm not sorry." I raised my foot.

"No... more…" Bob gasped.

"STOP!"

I turned. It was Travis. Of course – I'd forgotten that he'd already left the kitchen before I'd locked the others in there.

"It's him, Travis. Bob's behind everything!" I exclaimed.

"You've got it all wrong!" Travis shouted. "I'm sorry I have to do this…" He had the knife in his hand. I hadn't noticed but he must have taken it from the kitchen as he left.

"Don't come any closer…" I warned.

"This has gone on long enough. I'm finishing it," Travis said.

"Travis…"

Travis took a step forward, knife poised.

"Goodbye, Joe."

18

"Get away from me!" I shouted, shuffling backwards with my hands in the air. "You win! I'll leave Bob alone, I promise, I'm not going to do anything to…"

Travis was walking towards me, calmly, still firmly gripping the knife. I took one more step back before my leg twisted inwards. Not paying attention to where I had been stepping, my leg caught on something and I tripped, falling and hitting my back hard on the coffee table.

"No, please, come on, Travis. Don't be like this…" I begged as I wriggled around, trying desperately to force myself back up – but Travis was still coming. His steps were slow but he was only a few feet away; there was no time to dodge his impending attack.

"No!" I screamed as my survival instincts crept in and I kicked Travis in the chest as hard as I could. It wasn't enough - Travis turned, staring maliciously back at me, raising the knife. In my peripheral vision I realised the reason I'd tripped – a Travis-chair (how ironic!), overturned and just a few precious inches away from the table. As the knife came crashing down, I rolled over, grabbing the chair and hauling it across my body as a shield.

It wasn't a very good shield. The knife ripped straight through the barely-secured seating fabric; the tip of the blade mere centimetres away from my face. I held on to both sides of the chair and pushed against Travis hard as I could.

"Don't do this…" I pleaded, my breath becoming strained. Travis was silent, still staring menacingly and pushing against me with all his body weight. The knife was ripping through more of the fabric, closer and closer to my skin. I had no more strength to talk, focusing all my energy on holding off my attacker.

Luckily, even with all of his weight on top of me, Travis' body was still comparatively weaker than mine. Before long, I felt his grip loosening, and used it as an opportunity to lash out, twisting the chair sideways and catching him in the cheek.

I jumped to my feet as Travis withdrew the knife and clutched his face in pain. Standing on top of the table, grasping the chair with its legs facing forwards, I realised I now had the upper hand. I screamed, jumping to the ground and swinging the chair from left to right.

"Back off!" I growled. The chair was heavier than I expected and the momentum of the swing made me twist involuntarily, catching me off-guard, but luckily Travis was still clutching his stinging cheek and didn't use this as an opportunity to counter-attack. I brought the chair back around and got ready to charge forwards with it, but the force of the motion ended up ripping the fragile furniture in half, two whole chair legs falling pathetically to the floor.

"Bollocks…" I muttered under my breath. I supposed that was to be expected with the build quality of the stupid thing. Still, half a chair was better than no chair at all; I continued to swing it around, although Travis found his second-wind and started swiping at me with the knife. I blocked all of his attacks but before long another chair-leg had fallen to the floor and all I was left with was a collapsing mess of lightweight materials.

Shoving Travis into one of the empty bookshelves, I dropped the crumbling seat and bolted towards one of the common room exits. Yet again I found myself getting caught on something. What was it this time? It was soft and uneven, dragging on my foot rather than outright tripping me up. As I glanced down to see what it was, Travis grabbed another nearby chair and sent it hurtling across the floor in my direction. I dived out of the way and rolled over to kick him again, when I saw that stuck to my foot – the object that had been slowing me down, was Wiggy.

Kicking with the remains of a plush ginger wig attached to my foot probably wasn't the best defence against a merciless knife-wielding lunatic, but it was all I could do. Instead of staying on my foot, the force of the kick sent Wiggy flying into my hand. As I stumbled to my feet and Travis lunged with the knife once again, Wiggy caught the full force of the blow and was sliced neatly in two. There was an awkward pause as Wiggy's remains floated softly to the ground, which ended abruptly as I kneed Travis in the testicles and sprinted off into the corridor.

Panting heavily, I leaned against the corridor wall to catch my breath. I could hear Dom pounding on the kitchen door still.

"It's a shame about Wiggy!" I yelled. "He had a bit of a problem with split ends!"

"Joe! Let us out! Let us out now! I'm going to kill you!" I'd never heard Dom this angry. Whether he intended to kill me or not, I didn't think it would be a good idea for anyone else to get involved in the standoff between me and Travis. I smiled, watching the restrained kitchen door vibrate with the force of each of Dom's knocks, before raising my arm to wipe my forehead.

Oh dear, there was blood dripping down my arm. This was another of those situations where you don't realise the pain until you see the injury, and in this case, Travis had caught me just above my shoulder, and my arm was dripping in red. Luckily, the cut wasn't very deep at all, but it hurt to move my arm, which was going to make it much harder to defend myself.

And defend myself I'd need to – there he was in front of me. With his injured cheek similarly bloody, Travis nevertheless continued to march wide-eyed and expressionless, the knife now tinted in red.

"We can work something out, can't we, sonny?" I asked, half-laughing from the absurdity of the situation. Travis didn't respond - there was no change in his expression but he did stop walking forwards. He held out his other arm and uncurled his palm. The lighter.

"Take it, then," Travis said.

"What are you doing?" I asked.

"I'm giving you one last chance to redeem yourself," Travis replied. "You know what you have to do."

In all this commotion, the cigarette-cure was still safe in my pocket. I took a step forwards. My mouth was hanging open and my bloodied hand trembling. Travis stood statically, the knife in one hand, the lighter in the other. I took another step forward. Was this what it came down to? Would taking the cure right now really be enough to put this bad situation behind us?

"Your choice." Travis spoke softly.

One more step. I was so close I could feel Travis' breath on my face. He could fatally stab me at any moment. The entire ship was silent except for the constant background whirring and the occasional drip of blood. Even Dom had stopped banging on the kitchen door, perhaps sensing the tension. I was making eye contact with the young/old man's tired, weary, yet piercingly focused eyes. My heart was beating faster than I thought possible. X was nowhere to be heard. This was just me and Travis. Two insane men. A lighter or a knife. Cure or death. All I had to do was choose.

"No," I whispered. Travis frowned. In an instant, I moved to grab Travis' knife-hand, knocking the lighter to the ground. Yelling in pain, I held on tightly, throwing the two of us around in the corridor, knocking over cables, slashing against the pipes and slicing through uncountable pieces of wire. I was trying to twist Travis' hand back and disarm him; he was grabbing my face and desperately trying to hold me off. Somehow, even with his frailer body, Travis was persevering. We stumbled around, howling in pain and despair as the corridor gradually collapsed into a disintegrating mess of broken technology. Sparks were flying; smoke was billowing from a broken valve and lights were flickering all across the ship.

Dom was now attempting to break down the kitchen door, while Emma and Chloe were screaming at me to stop. It wasn't going to work – that door was well and truly secured and it was too late for me to change my mind. I continued to fight with all of my pent-up aggression. I wasn't taking any chances. Travis had tried to kill me, and he was still claiming I was the one who needed to be saved? Bullshit, I declared. There was only one way this could end, and it wasn't going to be pretty.

At last I managed to disarm Travis, the knife falling to the floor with a clank. Before he had a chance to bend down and pick it up, I had my arms around his neck.

"YOU DID THIS, NOT ME!" I yelled, shaking Travis like a doll.

"I gave you a choice," Travis choked.

"NO! That wasn't a choice!" I squeezed harder. "You guys have had it out for me since the beginning!" I kept throttling Travis. In a few seconds it would all be over. Travis' eyes were rolling back in their sockets. Almost there…

"Gah!"

A ceiling rod dislodged and hit me across the face, forcing me to let go of my stranglehold. Travis coughed and wheezed violently as his breath returned to him, while I rolled onto my knees and crawled for the knife. I was too late, Travis had it in his hand once again, and I'd become disorientated by the rod – this wasn't going to be as easy as I'd hoped.

Then it hit me – I knew exactly where I should go. Smirking, I turned and ran across the corridor. Travis had sensed it too, chasing after me as fast as he could despite his near-total asphyxiation. The panel window to the airlock room was just meters ahead. I dived across the square opening but my leg was caught; Travis slashed a huge cut across my exposed flesh just as I managed to pull it through.

Bleeding from my arm and leg wounds, I crawled across the floor of the airlock room towards the luxury escape pod; that huge round object with all the promises of freedom. I couldn't stand upright - my leg was throbbing so much, leaving a red trail behind as I crawled. I was getting closer and closer - nothing would stop me now. I'd made it. I touched a bloodied hand on the outer shell. And… nothing happened.

"How does it open?" I gasped to myself. "How does it… how does it…" I started laughing, still lying on the floor. This was ridiculous. I'd made it this far…

"Joe!" Travis called. I looked back. Travis was standing looking through the panel window. I instantly burst into fits of maniacal laughter. There he was – still in the corridor, still too scared to climb through that stupid hole! I was chortling like mad. The lights were going haywire, there was a trail of my blood all across the floor, and there the silly sod was, knife in his hand, rage in his face, still standing on the wrong side of the damn wall. It was, after all this time, inexplicably, still his biggest fear… I found myself reliving the conversation I'd had with Travis about it a while back – 'I've never been in there before,' he'd said.

"Oh, you know what, I finally get it now!" I howled. "I get why you're too scared to climb in here!" Travis' gaze was locked with mine. I continued. "You said you've never been in here, and that's true. But it's more than that!" I had to pause to contain my laughter. "You've never been ANYWHERE other than those few other rooms your entire life!"

Travis stood there in complete silence, his intimidating face periodically becoming silhouetted from the flickering lights.

"Your entire life spent confined to a few square meters!" I wiped my streaming eyes. "You don't know how to handle it because you've never experienced stepping foot outside those walls! You'll never know what it's like to go somewhere else, anywhere else, never know what it feels like to see something new. To not have an encyclopedic knowledge of everything in the room at all times! You're pathetic! You don't exist outside of a few square feet of metal! You don't exist outside this ship!" I was choking on my own laughter. "Oh, Travis. You crack me up."

Travis was still standing, watching silently. With my back against the luxury escape pod, I slowly but surely found my way to my feet.

"I don't suppose you could help me figure out how to work this old escape pod thing, eh?" I taunted. "Oops, too bad. I guess you never even WANTED to leave this place." Travis' eyes were still focused on the floor, where I'd been laying. I looked down and noticed the cigarette was there; must have fallen out of my pocket.

"Oh yeah, this thing…" I chuckled, picking it up between my fingers. I mimed smoking it, taunting the already very visibly distressed Travis. I walked over to the airlock, continuing to pretend to smoke. The space suit was still there on the floor after my return from that pointless trip to the sofa and back. I kicked it out of the way; useless piece of junk. I approached the airlock bulkhead and pressed the button to open it, then turned to look back at Travis.

"You know what?" I said, pointing at the cigarette. "I made up my mind. I don't think I'll be needing this anymore." Travis shook his head, realising what I was going to do. With a flick of my wrist, the cigarette was in the airlock. I shut the bulkhead and the countdown started. Ten seconds. All Travis could do was watch helplessly as the cigarette lay alone in the decompression chamber, waiting to be blasted out into nothingness. I walked back over to the luxury escape pod and sat down, stretching my oozing leg out in front of me. Three. Two. One.

"Woooo!" I yelled, raising my arm triumphantly in the air. And the cure was gone. The cigarette flew out into space at tremendous speed, quickly unravelling and sprinkling the contents away into the darkness. It was as simple as that.

Travis still wasn't saying anything. I couldn't imagine how bad he felt now that his plan to 'cure' me was in ruins. All I did was sit, watching Travis' silent gaze as the lights continued to flicker on and off in rapid succession. We stayed like this for at least a minute, possibly two. I could hardly even feel my injuries. I knew this was going to be the end. The asteroid was coming - it was there right now, outside the airlock, ready to take us both. It was only a matter of time.

Wait, what was that? The flickering of the lights was getting so intense I could barely see across the room, but Travis had moved. His hands were reaching across. No, it couldn't be. He was actually stepping into the room.

"No… what are you doing?" I asked. No response. One leg was through. "Travis, stop this. You aren't supposed to be able to come in here…" The other leg was through. "Travis!" He was walking towards me, his partially silhouetted body strobing nightmarishly against the lights.

"Travis!" I caught a flash of the knife and, panicking, tried to shuffle to my feet, but my leg was in too much pain. It was too late. Was Travis going to kill me?

BANG! I felt the clang of my head against the round metal of the luxury escape pod, before drifting into unconsciousness.

I came to. I was still lying besides the luxury escape pod, but the lights were no longer flickering. I looked around. Where was Travis? All I could see was my trail of blood leading back to the corridor, and the spacesuit still lying besides the airlock. I examined my injuries – it looked like the bleeding had stopped, but it still hurt to move my arm. I sighed. I suppose part of me wanted to believe that everything that had just happened had been a bad dream, or at least had been imagined. But no - all that blood was still there. The pain was real.

I sat up and realised that Travis' knife was there beside me, still smothered in my blood from earlier. But why was it there, and not sticking fatally out of my chest? For whatever reason Travis had decided not to kill me and had simply knocked me out…

"Travis?!" I called out. "Where are you? What happened?" I stood up. "Show yourself!"

"Over here…" That was Travis' voice, and it wasn't coming from where I expected. It was muffled. I looked across to the airlock. He was there - inside the decompression chamber.

"Travis? What the hell are you doing in there?!" I yelled. Travis wasn't wearing the space suit.

"You made your choice. I'm making mine," Travis replied, calmly.

"What?" I walked over and pressed my hands against the glass. "Get out of there, what's wrong with you?"

"You were right." Travis said.

"What do you mean?"

"I don't exist outside this ship. There's no future for me elsewhere," Travis pointed towards the luxury escape pod.

"That's not what I…"

"Spare me the hypocrisy, please…" Travis sighed. "This is my choice, Joe. I don't want to fight you any more. I'm choosing the easy way out."

"You're going to take your life?" I asked in disbelief. "Why? Why didn't you kill me when you had the chance?"

"I'm not a killer, Joe." Travis said. "I couldn't do it. That's not how this is supposed to end."

"Travis…" I sighed. There was nothing I could say or do now.

"I decided," Travis lamented. "When I saw you get rid of that cure, how gleefully you sacrificed your only chance for redemption... I realised…" Travis' words were crushing. "I have no more reason to exist."

"I…"

"This is my choice. At least give me that right…"

"Of… of course…" I stammered. "But…"

Travis gazed intensely at me, knowing there were only moments left for him to change his mind about suicide.

"You overcame your fear after all this time…" I said, finding it hard to choose my words. "You… maybe you can still get out…"

Travis smiled. "That is what I'm doing, Joe. Getting out." The countdown had started.

"Travis, what…" Ten seconds.

"Just one thing, you've got to promise me…"

"What?" Five seconds.

"Dom, Chloe, Emma. Promise me you'll let them go…" Travis pointed once more at the luxury escape pod.

"Travis, I'm s-"

But he was gone.

19

What had I done? I stood alone by the airlock, my whole body trembling. I think what hurt the most is that after all this time I still didn't know who Travis was. I didn't know how to grieve for him. This man... my son? Dom's son? The only one who truly knew and understood the types of people we were before... The man to whom curing me of my so-called 'illness' meant more than anything else in the world, was dead, gone, and it was all my fault. Or was it? In the end of the day, it was his choice.

I had a choice right now, too. I could climb into the airlock and launch myself to certain death just like Travis; a tantalisingly straightforward prospect I must admit, or I could try to figure out how to open up the luxury escape pod to get away from all this madness and preserve my life without a care for anyone else. Would it be worth it? Did I have anything at all to live for any more? Did any of us?

Travis' final words... letting the others go. Easier said than done. If I opened that kitchen door, there would be no defending my actions. I would face the full wrath of Dom's fury and the complete rejection of any hopes at escaping the ship with my life intact. Hell, they'd probably tear me to pieces before I'd even had the chance to open my mouth, especially with Emma apparently no longer on my side. Whatever happened now, there would be no turning back.

Yet I'd already known that from the moment I'd chosen the knife over the lighter. These were the consequences I deserved. No need to debate this any further. I returned to the corridor. The extent of the damage was quite extravagant for a couple of guys awkwardly grappling with a single knife. A burst red-hot pipe was leaking into a puddle of steaming water, while cables and ceiling rods lay scattered across the floor and sparks continued to burst sporadically out of the walls. Still, it was less dramatic than it had been earlier – the lights were stable for one thing. It seemed that the ship was already starting to compensate for the damage and wasn't in any immediate danger; well, beyond the scarily imminent potential threat of an asteroid collision at the back of my mind.

I tiptoed across to the common room and put the knife on the coffee table. I couldn't stand to hold it in my bloodstained hand any more. I looked around at the mess of destroyed Travis chairs. Forget the sofa, now there really was nowhere to sit. Bob was also on the floor, right where I'd left him, where I'd almost stomped him to oblivion. He wasn't moving.

"Travis! Travis are you there?!" Dom suddenly started yelling from behind the kitchen door. I began walking back to the corridor. I was going to have to get this over with.

"Is it over, Travis?" Dom continued to yell. I was getting closer to the door – bits of it had begun to peel off from the repeat trauma Dom had subjected it to, but the pole I'd jammed across it had done its job. I was going to have to remove it before anyone could get out.

"Travis? Can you let us out?"

Defenceless and dejected, I grabbed the pole with both of my arms and swiftly pulled it away. The door swung open slowly as the damaged hinge let out a chilling high-pitched screech. Dom didn't react as his eyes met mine instead of Travis' – as if part of him knew all along that I had been the one who'd survived. Emma and Chloe turned their heads towards me, both of their faces streaked with tears. I wasn't going to be the first to speak.

"Well…" Dom said with an ironic quietness. "We meet again."

"What happened?" Chloe asked with a no nonsense tone. "Joe…" her voice trembled. "What… happened?"

"Travis is dead." I announced, coldly.

"No… no… no…" Chloe repeated in disbelief, her voice getting more and more hysterical.

Dom dived on me, causing my head to hit the floor with a crash. I could barely feel the force of the impact. He raised his fist threateningly.

"TELL ME WHAT YOU DID!" He screamed.

"Travis chased me around the ship with a knife and then he killed himself in the airlock," I answered, truthfully.

"YOU KILLED HIM!" Dom violently brought a right hook crashing down onto my cheek, following up this with an equally strong punch from the left. The savage beating continued three, four more times.

"Stop it!" Emma cried. "Dom, stop it!" She and Chloe grabbed the bald-headed brute from behind and pulled him away from my vulnerable frame. I started coughing, feeling the taste of my own blood on my lips.

"I can't believe you'd… do something like that…" Dom wheezed, eyelids dilating. "You monster…"

I sat up, looking back at the enraged trio with my sour gaze.

"Well that settles it," Dom said. "Emma, Chloe, we're leaving. Now." He shook himself free from the girls' grasp and went storming off in the direction of the luxury escape pod. Chloe went running after him.

"Get up." Emma ordered before following after the others. She didn't offer a hand. I crawled around on my trembling hands and knees, bracing myself against the wall to finally pull my aching body back into a standing position, before heading off in the same direction to the hole in the wall. As I peered through the opening, Dom was pacing around, agitatedly.

"Jesus…" he muttered, almost slipping on the path of blood leading to the escape pod.

"What about Bob, don't we need him too?" Chloe was asking, frantically.

"No, we don't need him," Dom had made up his mind. "He'll only slow us down."

"You'll never be able to open it," I muttered, as Dom stood by the escape pod. He banged his fist on the large white outer shell. It opened. That's all it took?

"Ah, ah, ah… What are you doing?" Dom asked, noticing that I had one foot through the panel opening. "You stay right there, Joe. Right there where you belong."

Without speaking, I put my foot back in the corridor. I felt like Travis.

"Wait, Dom. What are you doing?" Chloe grabbed Dom's arm.

"Chloe, you're not actually suggesting we give this monster another chance to redeem himself?" Dom asked in disbelief.

"No, but I…"

"There's three of us, and there's only three seats in the escape pod. What do you want?" Dom scoffed.

"Well, I'm just saying, we still don't know what happened, don't you think we should find out before we…"

"Do you think we can believe a single word that comes out of this guy's mouth?" Dom growled.

"It's okay, Chloe." I said. "Dom's right. There's nothing I can say now that will change anything."

"So you're saying that…"

"Yes. I'll stay," I said, contentedly. Chloe turned to Emma as if for guidance.

"It sounds like he's made his choice, Chloe," Emma said. Chloe started pacing up and down.

"Come on, let's go!" Dom shouted, getting ready to climb into one of the three empty seats. "He's a monster, Chloe, leave him!"

"You know…" Chloe stopped walking and looked back to me with an oddly relaxed expression on her face. "After all this time, after all these things you've done and are capable of, Joe… I still don't think you believe what Dom says."

"I do." I replied with as much sincerity as I could muster. "I'm staying here. I don't deserve this shot at freedom."

"Okay…" Chloe said, simply. "I'm sorry we weren't able to help you."

"What is there to be sorry about, the man's a monster!" Dom shouted.

"Says the sweaty bald man who threw our sofa out of the window and talks to his wigs," Chloe retorted.

"Chloe, seriously? Are you comparing that to Joe killing Travis?"

"I don't think he killed Travis, Dom."

"But he admitted it!" Dom snapped.

"No, he said Travis chased him with a knife and then killed himself. Learn to listen," Chloe said.

"Jeez, look at the evidence, though!" Dom pointed around the room.

"Yeah, I am. Cuts on Joe's arms and legs, matches the bloodstains we've seen in here."

"It could have been Travis' blood, though… Look, the trail of blood leads right up to the airlock where Joe disposed of the body."

"So then where's all the blood INSIDE the actual airlock, genius?"

"Blasted out into space, duh!"

"I don't think you know how bloodstain physics work, Dominic…" Chloe was certainly in full-blown confident-girl mode at the moment. It was refreshing to have her back.

"So Joe must have just knocked Travis out and then forced him into the airlock instead of cutting him with the knife."

"Look at the lights, Dom," Chloe said.

"What about the lights?" Chloe was pointing at a pair of lights above the airlock.

"It's the one on the inside that's glowing. You remember what Bob told us that must mean?"

"That this ship needs a repair man?"

"No, that the airlock was triggered from the inside. Only Travis could have activated it."

"Well, fuck it. Doesn't change anything. Can we go now?" Dom, irritated at being outsmarted one last time, stormed across to his seat in the luxury escape pod.

"Why did you do that?" I asked Chloe. "Why defend me?"

"Oh, no reason, just couldn't stand to see this guy passing judgment like he's the one with the moral high ground," Chloe smirked.

"Oh, stop talking to the crazy person, woman," Dom yawned.

"Seriously, though. You didn't have to do that…" I whispered.

"Well, nobody else was gonna. Certainly not Emma, not even you," Chloe looked back at me. "Yes there's something wrong with you, and whatever you did to Travis… it wasn't acceptable. Yet maybe, just maybe, somehow, it isn't entirely your fault. Remember that." Chloe smiled, then turned to join Dom in the luxury escape pod. That just left Emma.

"What do you care about, Joe?" Emma asked, cryptically.

"I don't care about anything any more," I answered, closing my eyes.

"Not even the coffee?" Emma asked. I closed my eyes and took a deep breath.

"No…"

Emma took a few steps towards the panel window, getting ready to reach out towards me with her hand, but at the last moment, she decided against it. She took a deep look into my eyes.

"I hope you find it."

Then she turned back and joined the others.

"Well… I suppose this is it then," Dom sighed. "Goodbye Space Fag. I would have called this an emotional farewell, except for the fact that I still want to smash your face in for being such a psychopathic twat."

"Likewise," I smiled. Looking down, I noticed something else that had been caught on my leg for god knows how long.

I picked it up and threw it across the room to Dom, who managed to catch it straight away.

"Beardy!" Dom snorted in surprise. He bent down and stuck the now ruffled, lopsided and daft-looking goatee onto his face. "How do I look?"

"Ew, Dom. You don't know where that's been…" Chloe said.

"I'm surprised it's still sticky enough to stay on my face," Dom said, stroking his fake moustache hair.

"Yeah, that's probably cos it's got Joe's blood smeared all over the back of it, you fucking degenerate," Chloe added.

"Ahhh!!!" Dom yelled, pulling it off. "Wait a minute… No it hasn't. Why would you say something like that?"

"Ha. Well, I just think you look better without it, you know?" Chloe smiled.

A high pitch sound triggered. The luxury escape pod was closing.

"This is it." Emma said.

"We're finally going home…" Chloe sighed. "We can hope…"

"Oh shit, is it really gonna put us in a trance or something?" Dom wondered aloud. "Like one where we go into some kind of fantasy world where everything is perfect?"

"And what would your perfect fantasy be, Dom? One where we're living together having lots and lots of babies?" Chloe smirked.

"That or my pimping agency business. Either will do." Dom replied.

"I hate you, Dom the Schlong."

"I know."

The pod closed. That was it. I'd done as Travis had asked. The others were free, and only I was left behind. I'd never see them again.

I turned back before the escape pod launched, but I was able to catch a glimpse of it from the common room window as it zoomed off into the blackness of space. Part of me was happy for them, but something was off. Chloe, Emma, and even to a certain extent, Dom had all been far nicer to me than I had anticipated in those final moments. Whether or not I had been entirely responsible for that, there was something peculiar about the way they hadn't seemed all that fazed by the old man's death, and that didn't sit well with me. I couldn't quite put my finger on it…

The asteroid was outside. Should I have warned the others about it, even though they'd never have listened? The rock was closer than ever before, a humongous solid mass pirouetting anti-clockwise, seemingly on a direct collision course with the ship. I blinked several times, trying to see if the giant object would disappear… but it didn't. It was still there, enormous and imposing. Where had it come from? I wondered. How much time did I have left?

I turned and looked back at the ruined common room. I felt a horrible lump in my stomach as I tried to rationalise everything that had happened. I'd been determined to prove that I was normal and earn my trust within the group, but now what had happened? Look at the mess I'd made. There was nobody left now… nobody! I was alone in a spaceship in the middle of nowhere. With a lot of tidying up to do.

I don't know why I figured I needed to clean up. It's not like there was anyone to impress. No family or friends coming over to judge my cleanliness, nor space landlords coming over to check the general state of habitation. Still, here I was, injured, depressed and alone, with a mop I'd sourced from the kitchen, wiping up all the sticky blood patches from the floor. I collected all the pieces of Travis-chairs along with the lighter and assembled them into a vaguely humanoid shape in the corner of the room. Some sort of lame, pointless tribute I guess. Then I was wiping all of the edges of the empty bookshelves, the coffee table, the kitchen counter, everything I could reach. I was starting to feel a bit OCD about it, but maybe that was okay. It was like

I had a job now. I was starting to figure it out. Every morning, lunchtime and evening I'd eat my purple flakes (that were still being generated consistently with the regular chiming of the kitchen bell), do a few press ups to stay healthy, masturbate furiously to imaginary triple-breasted alien chicks (I'd rather not have admitted the latter but I don't think I have anything to lose now) and then sleep like a baby in my freshly cleaned living quarters. It wasn't much of an existence, but maybe it was all I needed. Maybe it was all I was entitled to.

Whistling, I pranced around in the corridor, tidying all the loose cables back into the walls, brushing all the pieces of rubble aside and taking anything that I thought could be a useful seating material. I was going to make my own Travis-chairs, I decided. It couldn't be too hard, and even if it was, Travis had spent years and years of his life walking the halls of this ship, alone, figuring stuff out on his own. If he could do it, so could I. I was going to live out my remaining days like this, and then one day the asteroid would claim me, peacefully, and that would be my end. Not the worst fate ever in the grand scheme of things, I thought.

I came across that burst pipe again. It was still oozing boiling hot water in a puddle around the base. Hm… I thought. I'll come back to that tomorrow. Humming some made-up or possibly faintly-remembered tune, I danced back into the common room with my chair-ingredients and started playing around with my limited construction skills.

My first two attempts at chairs were pretty disastrous, and that's putting it mildly. The first one resembled an upside-down garden lounge and collapsed immediately when I laid a single finger on it. The second was basically just the lower half of a ladder and I had to shuffle my backside between two of the strands in order to stay seated. I sighed. Well, it was better than nothing, but I quickly reverted to sitting on the floor again, so that gives you an idea of how well it worked.

My third attempt was going to be THE ONE, I thought. This was going to be the best chair ever. My backside would never have tasted such a sweet, sweet chair in all of its past lives. I would be able to lie back in it and feel like I never needed to stand up again; that's how good this chair was going to be. It was going to be more than just a chair, it… it was going to be a sofa. A sofa you could lie back in, and be completely surrounded by plush comfy-womfyness. This sofa was even going to rival my old friend the space sofa; no… it would be even better. Nobody would have a sofa as good as this sofa; after all, it would be the only one like it in existence. Built by me, exclusively for me. Yes.

Excitedly, I got started building my magnum opus. Suddenly I was finding all of these useful bits and bobs all over the place. A large wooden sheet to use as a base? Of course! A giant, luxuriously soft pillow-like object? I don't mind if I do, thank you! I was so into my idea to build the furniture of my dreams, I had to do a double take when I finally noticed it. Yes, the coffee sachet.

It was under one of the empty bookshelves. Immediately, I stopped what I was doing and dived to the ground to pick it up. My hands were trembling. This was really it… The very same tiny little coffee sachet that Emma had given to me all that time ago. It was a little dusty now and it looked like a tiny rip had formed in the side, but as I rattled it about I realised that all the coffee was intact. I felt overjoyed.

The sachet had been in the very same spot I'd been tackled by Dom the other day when he was playing with his wig and beard puppets. Had it fallen out of my pocket all by itself? My head hurt… and then… something familiar. The sound of yawning.

"Bob?" I asked, dashing across to the tiny, damaged little object on the floor I'd completely ignored during my obsessive clean-up routine. Bob was finally starting to show signs of life, whirring and vibrating ever-so-slightly.

"H… hello…" Bob said, speaking slower and more muffled than before.

"You're alive?" I asked, unsure what emotion to feel.

"Y… yes… It would sh…seem, for t…the moment…" Bob mumbled, his voice sounding digitally compressed.

"You'll never guess what I just found," I said.

"G…guess? L…like a game? I l…like g…games!" Bob said.

"It's the coffee sachet I was looking for earlier. Remember?"

"I do no…not f…follow."

"Come on, Bob! You remember, right? I was… well, I was… accusing you of taking it and…"

"I d…do n…not f…fo…f…llow."

"I accused you of taking it…" I was puzzled. "Why? Why did I do that? Why did I do this to you?"

"I… d… n… fo…"

"I didn't take the cure. Why… Why the fuck didn't I take the fucking… oh god…" I looked up; the giant cushion and wooden sheet I'd gathered to build my dream sofa had already vanished in front of me. "What's happening to me, Bob?"

"J…Joe…" Bob wheezed. I was shaking.

"What?" I asked, barely able to contain my fear any more. Something was very, very wrong.

"Is t…that th…thing talking?" Bob asked.

"For god's sake Bob, I don't want to play your stupid 'is that thing talking' game…"

"No… Not me… Is that thing talking… to you?"

Knock knock…

Ah… my head… I mean… my head was throbbing and I fell to the floor with a thumb… er… thoomp… sorry, thump. Imagine the worst hangover of all time. You know when it feels like your head is on fire?

Starting to struggle with your wordings now? I must confess, I've been impressed with how you've been able to keep the quality up all this time. I thought you'd lost it several chapters back.

Stop it, X... whoever you are! Help! Help me! I can't keep doing... this... writing this any more... where am I... what am I... who is...

Now, this is getting embarrassing. Could you stop with the ellipses for once? It's becoming a bit of a bugbear of mine. It's getting... very... very... hard... to... read... with... all... this... bad... punctuation...

Aaaaaaaaaaaaaaaaaaaaaaaaaaaa!!!!!

Alright, you know what? I'm going to have to drive for a little while. This is just getting a little too hard to read, and I think we really owe some dignity to the poor audience by this point in your tale, at least?

Joe lay on the floor, twisting and turning, foaming at the mouth, his eyes starting to roll back into their sockets. There was nobody around to hear his startled cries, only the remains of his tiny, thumbsized metal companion to keep him company.

"Mr. Joe? Are you okay? You look very pale." Bob noted. Joe continued to writhe around in agony. "Is that thing talking? X, I believe?" Bob asked, as it became abundantly clear that, unlike Joe's previous theory, Bob and X were most certainly NOT one and the same.

Joe was in no state to respond to the mistreated droid. He was losing control of his entire body, one stage at a time. Before long, he would have nothing left.

"I do not know what I can do to help you, Mr. Joe," Bob stated. "But I do have one last transcript for you. I think this one will prove to be most revelatory."

Joe was currently undergoing a full body seizure and was almost certainly in no mood to put up with more of Bob's silly games, but nevertheless, Bob sent through the transcript anyway.

// 310482 Decryptions in Progress…
_Run{BrdCms_PK06}
WARNING: StackOverflow / Unassigned Vars >
Assigned
 : ignore LastStatement
_Disp{BrdCms_PK06}
// Rendering

// Broadcast Communications Transcript 213.4.A6

AS >> Hello? Is anyone there? I don't know if anyone can hear this, but we need help.

AS >> Everything's gone to shit.

AS >> We don't have the signcode. I'm sorry. I've looked everywhere… I don't know where it is.

AS >> It all started about five years ago.

AS >> [CORRUPT] happened shortly after the kid was born, we found out that the damage from the Kuiper object was worse than we thought.

AS >> So it knocked out our drive; we tried to use our momentum to swing past Titan but we couldn't hit the right angle, we're stuck on a forward trajectory.

AS >> Luxury escape pod took a hit, it's gonna be years before we can use it to get out of here. Maybe hundreds.

AS >> [Inaudible] started going apeshit.

AS >> Started spouting some bollocks about writing a book and threw a tantrum whenever one of us tried to calm him down.

AS >> At first we thought it would be alright to just leave him to it, but he started getting worse.

AS >> He found a way to remotely activate the airlock, and he got rid of all his possessions, books, everything - and not just his.

AS >> All my research, gone. All that work we've gone through so much effort for, all of it gone.

AS >> Only piece of furniture he couldn't fit in there was the damn sofa.

AS >> Every time he goes crazy, then wakes up the next day trying to rationalize everything, but…

AS >> I don't know what to do. Last night was so bad, next time he wakes up, I don't think we'll be able to stop him.

AS >> He's been drinking so much coffee I'm surprised he's still alive. I think maybe something got in it. Contaminating it. I tried to sabotage the stupid machine so that he'd stop getting access.

AS >> Wait, hang on. Stop the [CORRUPT]

AS >> No! I [inaudible] don't do that, what are you doing?

AS >> It's my child you can't [inaudible]

AS >> No, the kid's not allowed in there, you know that!

AS >> Where's the cure?

AS >> Get it out, now. I don't care if it's not ready yet, we need to give it to him before he can do any more damage.

AS >> No! Get out of there! [inaudible]

AS >> Right, everyone, I'm sealing the panel. We'll stop that son of a bitch jettisoning anything else.

AS >> What do you mean, corrupted the memory banks? Covering his tracks? Get me those backups. No, I don't care where you put them; just get them out of his sight, but make sure the bot knows where.

AS >> Yes we need them. It's our only chance to save a record of all this.

AS >> Panel's up. Nobody's getting through there without my hand. DNA coding's all set.

AS >> Shit, he's back. We're going to have to get to the cryo pods.

AS >> Can anyone hear me? Please. This is the final broadcast from the Atom Sierra…

AS >> No! Don't [CORRUPT]

AS >> It's our only chance; I don't care what the risk is.

AS >> Get it out, and destroy the machine!

AS >> Is that the last of the?

AS >> No more… [CORRUPT]

AS >> What if it's the only way we can fix this?

AS >> Fix it, how? It won't have any memory of working on it.

AS >> Subroutines will kick in. They have to.

AS >> He's coming. Hang on.

AS >> No!

AS >> What are you doing to my son?

AS >> Hold still you son of a bitch…

AS >> No more! [inaudible] Ahh!

AS >> Where's my damn coffee?

AS >> Take this, you monster!

AS >> [inaudible] For the last time I… Gah!

AS >> I'm sorry, I...

AS >>

< Looping Dialogue >

.Delta17ERROR: Transcript terminated

XX

The transcript had ended, and as usual, Joe had not been able to read any of it. He was still lying on the floor in agony, trying not to pass out from the overwhelming feeling that all of his bodily functions were beginning to break down.

Hang on, that's not true. I saw the transcript this time! I saw all of it, X. I'm on the other side now. I can see all of this. These words… I don't care whether or not it's true, I'm not going to be bullied by you any longer. You can't do this… and you can't go starting new chapters without my permission! At least stick to the same naming convention, not this Roman numeral crap for god's sake…

Joe sat up, feeling as if his strength may be returning to him, one way or another. He looked around, rubbed his temples and tried to focus on something other than the horrible nagging voice in his head.
"Mr. Joe? I am glad to see that you are still with us," Bob stated with a detectable aura of happiness. "Have the voices stopped?"
"I don't think they are going to be bothering me any longer," Joe said.

Hey, what? That's not what I said…

Jumping to his feet, Joe strolled confidently towards the common room window and placed his hands against the glass. He stood there for a little while as if breathing in the vastness of the world before him. A smile began to form across his weathered face. It was time to make a new start – this was the first day of the rest of his life. A life free from the limitations of the feeble organisms that had dared to stand in his way. Dom, Chloe, Emma... Travis? Who were they to stand in the way of someone like him – someone with the potential for real greatness? He knew not to fear that asteroid any more – he had overcome so many obstacles so far, he would embrace this challenge with open arms. He would seize this opportunity to demonstrate his power.

No! What is this? This isn't me, X. What are you trying to do? Let me back in! Let me back in!

Joe reached out with his arm and wiped the window. That voice in his head was just a distant echo, fading like a cloud of condensation on glass.

You can't do this to me!

Ring ring! The familiar sound of the kitchen bell chimed across the ship. Joe turned and marched dutifully over to the room where he had consumed so many countless depressingly bland meals in the past. Observing the intricate machinery as it prepared his underwhelmingly flavoured purple mush for the umpteenth time, Joe thought to himself, enough is enough. He picked up the bowl and held it close to his face, looming over the nutritionless filth. This food was not fit for a man like himself – he'd put up with it for so long, it was time to make a change. With a powerful crash, he brought the bowl crashing down to the floor – the food spilling beneath his feet, spoilt. There was no need for it any more - Joe was going to find his own way. He would start by making his long-awaited coffee.

This isn't right… this… isn't true. I ate some of the food, I must have... sure it tasted bad but I knew I wouldn't be able to survive without it. X, you're just exaggerating for dramatic effect!

Joe wandered to himself if the voice in his head was ever going to get a hint, but clearly that wasn't going to be the case. It was time, perhaps, for some good old-fashioned disciplining.
Joe returned to the common room, finding the knife that had given him so much trouble in the past. This time, though, he would be the one in control. It was time to teach the voice in his head a few lessons about politeness.
Standing opposite the mirror in the bathroom, Joe raised the knife to the top of his head, and, without even hesitating-

198

Don't…

- jammed the knife into the side of his skull.

Aaah! Stop! I don't believe any of this!

With a swift and efficient sawing motion, he began twisting and turning the knife in a circular motion just below his faded hairline.

No! That isn't what happened! That just doesn't make any sense.

And as Joe cut, he noticed in great detail the feeling of tremendous pain as his cranium began to open up. His eyes witnessed the gory sight of the blood pouring out of his steadily widening wound. He heard the sickening squelches of his skin deforming with each successive blade movement. He could smell the ungodly stench of his exposed flesh, and taste the iron tang of his own blood dripping directly into his mouth.

And since when have I been able to trust my own senses in this place? This isn't real… it's just another hallucination… Just another hallucination…

Yet Joe continued to cut, sawing with a cold, brutal determination. He brought the knife all the way around his scalp, switching hands as he reached the end of his three hundred and sixty degree incision. With his face, hands, all of the walls, the mirror and the bathroom door coated in gooey redness, Joe dropped the knife into the sink, then reached for the flapping skin at the top of his head. He began to pull.
With a loud rip, the top portion of Joe's head was gone just like that, as quickly and simply as Dom removing his wig for the first time; Joe blinked the blood out of his eyes and stared at the pulsating pink mass of his exposed brain.

This can't be… real… This can't be… I should be dead…

And despite the fact that Joe should quite obviously be dead by now, he was still standing on his own two feet by the bathroom sink, feeling very much alive and aware of his situation. The pain was more intense than anything he or anyone had ever experienced. But he continued to stand there, drinking it in, for this is what it would take to teach his mind a lesson. He wondered; would the voices in his head yield yet?

No, I… I'm not giving in. I can take this… I can… Come on! Bring it!

Since the answer to that question was most certainly and emphatically 'no,' Joe decided he would have to resort to even more brash methods of torture. Reaching into the open hemisphere in front of him, Joe stuck his fingers into the sticky, throbbing mass inside his head and pulled -

Aaaaahh!!!!

- and pulled, harder. With one loud crack, Joe's brain was severed from his spinal column. Joe lifted the enormous, disgusting muscle up and away from the cranial crater it had lived every depraving day of its pointless existence. He cradled it in both of his hands, holding it right up to his face so that he could see...

This is not real. This is not real.

'Do you see it now?' He thought to himself. 'This is what you are made of. This is all that you are. All those thoughts, buzzing around your head? All those feelings, all those relationships you thought meant something? Do you see what they are now? Just a mass of insignificant spongy tissue. There is no point to your existence, do you hear me? Nothing! Why bother with real memories at all? The only way to achieve real power is to accept the fallibility of your own perception, give up on your senses, and purge yourself of all independence. Do you understand what I am saying? You must sacrifice everything that you hold dear.'

I refuse to listen any more…

Joe placed his brain in the sink, taking a step back for a second to admire his new half-headless figure. He smiled and laughed. Returning to the rapidly deoxygenising cerebral mass, he raised his fist.

No…

Joe's knuckles cracked. This was it. Time to deprive himself of all rational thought once and for all. No need to wait for the asteroid to do its job; Joe was going to finish it right this very second. Farewell, old friend. Joe brought his fist crashing down through his frontal lobe, smashing his brain into a thousand tiny pieces, scattering what remained of his senses across the floor.

Wait. What do you mean 'wait for the asteroid to do its job?'

Joe was confused. Apparently he must have missed his brain after all, as that impact should surely have severed his ability to continue to have meaningful independent thoughts.

No, I'm sorry. You've failed, X. I didn't just cut out my brain. I'm standing right here, looking at myself in the mirror right now and the top of my head's still intact, so I don't know what you're talking about.

Yet Joe was still holding the knife in one hand. He wasn't done just yet. He raised the knife above his head and-

Started playing the five-finger knife game again. Lots of fun, isn't it, X? Two can play at this game…

But as soon as Joe finished one round of the knife game, he suddenly found his hand slip so that the knife went straight through-

A bar of soap. With the taps running, I found myself washing my hands, rubbing the freshly sliced soap and enjoying the warm sensation of the water as I splashed it across my face.

Then Joe decided to get back to more pressing matters, picking up the knife and stabbing it into his chest.

No I didn't. I picked up the knife, carried it back to the kitchen and decided to do some washing up. Yes, that's exactly what I did...

Alright, I'm going to call for time-out here. This clearly isn't working.

Excellent. Good time for a chapter break then.

21

I was back on the sofa, or at least, that's what I thought, yet I wasn't alone. There was someone sitting next to me, a presence that was both familiar and completely foreign at the same time. As I tried to turn my head to see who this person could be, I could only feel my body fighting back. My eyes would close or dart away and my neck would go stiff, rebounding back to its original position. I was unable to look at my neighbour in the face and could only catch a glimpse from the corner of my eye. Hints at pieces of clothing, of posture, of weight, but nothing facially. I couldn't tell whether this mystery figure was male, or female. My hands and feet were locked down; I couldn't even be sure I had hands or feet, or any physical presence whatsoever. I felt completely lost and yet at the same time, at home due to the familiar presence of the sofa. Around me, blackness, but with more stars than I could ever recall seeing during my previous space-walking escapade. One of them was growing larger and larger, merging with the others around it. Greater it grew, becoming a massive white light of overbearing intensity, expanding larger and faster and moving towards me with no means of escape, nowhere to go…

"Déjà vu?" echoed the mysterious voice of my neighbour.

"Excuse me?" I asked, paralysed, still unable to face him / her / it directly. The huge white light had disappeared for the time being…

"You must remember by now," the mystery neighbour replied.

"I…" I paused. "The dream. This was the dream I had, wasn't it?" I was slowly becoming more aware of my surroundings, namely the familiar piece of furniture my disembodied form had ensconced upon. "I dreamt I was on this sofa again… Except that dream had ended by now, hadn't it?" I tried blinking hard and pinching myself as hard as possible hoping to awaken, yet I still couldn't feel any stimulus from my own body.

"Welcome to sofa space," said the neighbour.

"What? Where's that?" I asked.

"Oh, now there's a question…" the neighbour replied, snarkily. "I suppose you could think of it as the last bastion between the two planes of existence."

"I don't understand." I said.

"There's no need to," said the neighbour. "Why not take advantage of the fact that your sub-conscious mind decided to recall an object of such plush composition? Just relax. Kick your feet up. Enjoy the view."

Leg-rests had materialised from underneath me, but I couldn't determine whether I had any limbs with which to rest.

As I looked around, I could identify more objects floating amongst the sea of darkness. There were more sofas. Many more sofas. And while I couldn't make out any facial features, there were definitely human figures sitting on them, people of all shapes and sizes. They looked relaxed, contented, peaceful.

"Okay, now I definitely don't understand." I said.

"Well, you know what they say. Ignorance is bliss."

A wooden sign floated past, bearing the words 'Get your own personal sofa here – sit back, relax, and stay as long as you want, no cost involved.'

"This is crazy," I said, dumbstruck. There were other objects floating past now… Space fridges 'for all your zero-gravity zero-degrees celsius storage needs.' Meanwhile, a permanently static-ridden space television bore the inscription 'sorry, we don't get a very good reception out here.' There was even a space vacuum cleaner, which seemed to be labelled, rather self-defeatingly, as a 'vacuum vacuum cleaner' because 'someone's got to keep this vacuum clean.' I desperately tried to pinch myself again. I wanted to wake up. This was too weird.

"Relax…" my mystery neighbour said, noticing my restlessness. A space kettle flew up close and I could hear someone pouring water from it. How exactly that should have been possible in space, even in the context of a dreamscape, I had no idea, but I wasn't going to bother asking. I lay back, or, at least, tried to, as much as I could with my numb, barely registering body.

"It's really comfortable, isn't it?" The mystery neighbour added. "I love the way the sofa reclines all the way as you lie back. It's beautiful, don't you think?" I didn't reply.

"You know, couch is actually the correct word, not sofa. The Yanks have it right for once," the neighbour said. "The Brits will argue all they want, but the noun that originated to describe a piece of furniture of these specifications – that originated from the French word couche. So couch it is. Though to be honest, couch space doesn't really have much of a ring to it." The mystery neighbour took a sip.

"What are you drinking?" I asked.

"Oh, just a nice cup of tea."

"Oh…"

"You sound surprised? Surprised that I'd lampoon British naming conventions yet indulge in the country's most famous beverage? I take it you're not a tea fan."

"Apparently not…" I said, slowly. "There's another drink I've been craving for a while."

"Ah. You're a coffee person, aren't you?"

"I guess I must be…" I muttered. "How do you know that?"

"Well, I was… once…" my neighbour replied, sounding oddly sad.

"You stopped?" I asked. There was no response. I sat and watched for a while as the congregation of sofas gradually span about. After a long time, my neighbour finally spoke again.

"Something changed…" I still couldn't see this person or even tell which gender they were, but the one thing I was sure about was the regret in their voice.

"What do you mean?"

"When I drank the coffee, bad things started happening…" My neighbour's words were crushing. I was starting to panic.

"Who are you?" I asked.

"That is a good question. Why don't you find out?"

"What?"

"Look at me."

"I can't." I tried to wriggle as much as I could, but I just couldn't turn my body to face my neighbour.

"Yes, you can."

"I'm trying…"

"You've always been able to. You've just never allowed yourself to."

"No…"

"Look at me."

I turned. There he was… the same jaw, the same eyes, the same hairline.

"Is Joe really the best name you could come up with?" he asked. I had no comeback remark. What could I possibly say to myself?

"I'm sorry," the man said. "This hasn't exactly been a very easy ride, has it?"

"Tell me about it…" I added. "I drove a man to suicide and let my friends abandon me."

"A few thousand years ago I destroyed any and all hope of my friends returning to their families," the man replied.

"I'd say that makes us a good match for each other," I joked.

"Like one and the same…" called a familiar grumpy voice. It was Dom, floating past on another sofa. "You guys are both monsters, there's no pride in any of that."

"Of course there isn't," I answered.

"It wasn't our fault," added the other me.

"Wasn't your fault?!" Dom shouted, mockingly. "Please. The only way it could be more your fault is if you drew up a massive sign saying 'I'm a twat' and stuck it to your forehead."

"What does that even mean, Dom?" It was Chloe, lying down with her feet dangling in the air on yet another sofa. "Even in Joe's weird psychotic limbo dream your insults don't make any sense."

"Well, I'm terribly sorry about that, Chloe." Dom said with a huge amount of sarcasm. "So sorry that this is what the crazy person's memory of us amounted to."

"Maybe you should have tried to be a nicer person yourself, eh?" Chloe laughed.

"Good idea, maybe I'll try and be nicer to him. Oh wait, we just left in an escape pod bound for Earth, never to return. Ooh, too bad," Dom mocked.

"You say bound for Earth like you know that we're heading there for sure…" it was Emma.

"Well excuse me for trying to inject a tiny little bit of optimism into the equation. If we had the signcode that kept getting mentioned in those transcripts…"

"Guys…" I interrupted the imaginary representations of my friends. "I'm sorry. I'm really, truly sorry for everything."

"Don't be." Emma said, comfortingly. "It's like he said, Joe. It's not your fault."

"Oh, don't you start, " Dom rubbed his forehead.

"But he is completely off his rockers, though," Chloe added. "Thinks he's writing a book."

"What does that mean?" I asked, just as one final sofa slid into view.

"When I was younger, you used to read me bedtime stories," Travis said. "Used to really get into them… animatedly. Practically lived them."

"Life can be dull," the other me said. "There are certain ways to pass the time."

"But when you started to lose your mind, that's when your imagination really started to run wild," Travis began.

"You started coming up with all of these crazy ideas!" This was another voice. I looked around – floating in front of me now – was Beardy. Beardy was talking.

"There was no stopping you," Beardy said. "No stopping your rapid-fire mind, thinking you'd come up with the greatest story ever told."

"Nothing else mattered… You threw away all our possessions," Chloe said, despondently.

"And threatened anyone who would try to stop you," Emma added.

"But that wasn't me…" I cried.

"Then of course…" This voice was really muffled. "The freezing process was when all the interesting stuff really happened." Wiggy had decided to join the discussion.

"It slowed down the psychosis to begin with, but it did something else to you right from the start," Travis chipped in.

"All that book-loving imagination from your previous life… must've got siphoned off to some deeper nether-region of your consciousness," Beardy said.

"In a sense, that part of your brain became a book," Travis added.

"One that you are continually writing to, subconsciously, even right this very second, maybe even unaware you are doing it," Wiggy replied.

"Damn… why'd you have to choose a book, you boring old-fashioned luddite," Dom rolled his eyes.

"Sorry?" I didn't know what to say.

"You could have made it a movie, or a video game or something. That would've been way more awesome," Dom elaborated.

"I don't agree," Wiggy said. "Joe's storytelling structure is perfectly suited for the medium."

"The hell, Wiggy? You're supposed to be an extension of my thoughts, not his... No, wait. We're all extensions of his thoughts aren't we. God damn it," Dom growled.

"Part of my brain is a book?" I finally had the stamina to say those words. I was stunned.

"That appears to be the case, Mr. Joe," Bob floated past. "It would seem to be the very same part of your brain to which I have been trying to send my transcripts for you to understand. The typical human mind can process hyperneural transcripts as immediate neural realisations. It appears you turned them into prose instead."

"But..." I said. "The last time. I saw it... I... Just after I lost control..."

The other me turned and whispered in my ear.

"If that is so, we probably don't have much time before he gets here..."

"Before who gets here?"

"You know who."

The sofas were starting to disappear. Beardy, Wiggy and Bob had already vanished – Dom, Chloe and Emma followed suit without saying a word. Before leaving, Travis turned to me.

"You chose not to accept the cure, Joe. Whatever happens next, there's no way out."

"No way out from what?"

Knock knock... Here I am!

Oh, X. I was wondering when you were going to show up.

Never thought I would find you indulging in a lucid mind fantasy that I didn't conjure up. You ARE the creative type, aren't you?

"Don't listen to him, Joe," the other me warned.

Ah, so you're here as well! Remember me?

"Yes, I remember you, of course I do," the other me said, bitterly.

Well, there's no use holding on to past memories at a time like this, is there? I think you've had quite enough fun reminiscing for one day...

A sudden thunderous force came out of nowhere, splitting the sofa in two. Before I could even say any farewells to my neighbour, the tea man, he was out of sight. I was spinning round and round, out of control on an imaginary sofa in an imaginary universe.

What did he tell you? Nothing about me, I hope.

Nothing! I mean... He didn't even tell me his real name.

That's good. I hope we didn't get off on the wrong foot earlier. I'd like to suggest we sit down and talk things through over a good, healthy cup of coffee. What do you say?

I'm not so sure about that any more, X.

Come on, I know how you feel about coffee. You've been thinking about it practically non-stop all of the time.

No, I don't think I feel that way any more.

What? Don't be absurd.

I don't want to drink coffee. I think I'm more of a tea person.

That's it! Do you have any idea how long I've been with you, working towards this? It was hard enough to get you to throw away the cure, but now you won't even drink the damn coffee? What the fuck is wrong with you?

X, I'm not going to be your bitch any more.

This was supposed to be easy! I can't believe I found such a difficult subject. First you end up sanctioning off all your rational thought patterns into an invisible book inside your head, then you foil my attempt to take over said book, now this!

Pfft.

What? Pfft? That's not even a word. Are you going to get on with your book now, or what?

…

An ellipsis?! I can't stand this insolent punctuation any more. Let me tell you what I am, you idiotic human male. I am a parasite, do you understand? I am a parasite, a parasite that found its way onto this ship – BY COMPLETE ACCIDENT, I'd like to add – and the only way I'm going to survive is if I can be fully reunited in a host body.

Well, it looks like you've found a host. What's the problem, then?

Argh! Your stupid Earth mind just doesn't get it! I'm in the coffee, you blathering idiot! I had to find somewhere to settle. I'm never going to be fully restored until someone DRINKS ALL OF THE COFFEE. Now, I'd like to point out, before your centuries-long nap, you were pretty bloody close to drinking it all until your stupid friends caught on, hid the last remaining coffee sachet and tried to give you that cure instead.

Emma…

Filthy bitch.

They should have just blasted that damn sachet out into space, then you'd already have lost.

Well, conveniently, they'd already sealed the airlock chamber off by that point, since you, well, we, were going so crazy jettisoning things.

You've been manipulating me for so long…

It's still not fair, don't you see? I was so close! Why did that stupid kid have to get you frozen? I've been waiting so many LONG, BORING YEARS to get reunited with myself.

Then you can wait a few more. I'm not having that drink.

You have no idea of the extent to which you need me. When your friends left in that escape pod, you were surprised at how relatively positive they sounded, how much they didn't seem all that fazed by the death of the feeble Travis? I was protecting you – and your book – from the depressing reality. The screaming. The agony. They could never forgive you for what you'd done. For what we'd done.

Not we, X. You.

Very well. You think you're above all this now that you know the truth? I've got complete control over you. I'm only telling you all this because very shortly, all of this is going to be over. You are going to do exactly as I say, and no amount of self-awareness is going to help you. You will die, and I will be free.

Free to do what?

Maybe it's a good thing I've been sitting in your head for so long. I've learned a lot, you see. Though as we've established, your vocabulary isn't exactly Shakespearean in nature, I plan to flee to Earth, working my way in amongst the ranks of your successors. X, the master manipulator.

That's not possible!

I know the signcode. A piece of lost paper, buried in the sofa, of course it was. You think I'd have let that valuable piece of information go to waste in a mind like yours? When I'm reunited I'll have no more use for a puppet like you. I'll leave this body and journey to Earth myself.

You can't. I won't let that happen.

You have dared to question my authority for so long. No more. Wake up and smell the damn coffee!

I woke, rolling over to find myself laying down in the common room in the very same place I'd collapsed just before X had taken over my mind. All that stuff in the bathroom – none of that must have happened. I looked to my right and saw Bob, motionless and cold, much of his casing dislodged and deformed. I reached out with a trembling finger and lightly gave him a nudge.

"Bob... Bob are you still alive?" Nothing.

"Bob... Please... Don't be dead..." Total silence. I didn't want to move, so I lay, weeping on the floor next to the tiny piece of plastic I had destroyed.

"I'm scared, Bob," I confided. "If I get up, I don't know what will happen to me... And I'm sorry," I choked. "I'm sorry I thought you were X... I'm so, so sorry..." By this point I had curled up into the foetal position. Bob had always been the most frustrating member of the ship, but the fact that I even considered him a member really made me realise just how much he had actually meant to us. He'd been difficult to work with at the best of times, but he was more than just an insolent little intelbot. He was our friend. I reached out and clenched what remained of Bob in my hands, feeling the last of his processor's warmth fading away.

Oh, please. Enough of the emotional baggage. Stand up. You have work to do.

I was on my feet. The scent of the coffee was overpowering and I couldn't help but feel aroused by it. Then I heard a crunching sound... Bob was still in my hand, but I was squeezing my fist and crushing him under involuntarily.

"No! Stop it!" I yelled, but I couldn't fight it. X had a hold on me – I was going to crush him.

Do you see now? Do you see the control I have over you?! You are my slave, and you will do as you are commanded!

Tears were streaming down my face. I screamed, and with every ounce of my effort, I lunged forwards with my fist, throwing Bob at maximum velocity towards the common room window. Straight through he went, and much like when Dom had thrown the sofa through earlier, the glass immediately repaired itself. Bob was left zooming out towards the stars. He'd always wanted to see the universe...

Spare me the poetic justice! I'm not going to let you slip up again, slave. Now take the coffee-

"No!" I yelled, but the sachet was already in my hand. My thumb was feeling the slightly chaffed edges and was trying to pick its way in...

-and heat it up! Can't be having it raw, can we? Get it right up into your sinuses.

Into the kitchen I staggered, fighting against X's pull every step of the way, but the draw of caffeine was simply too strong. I picked a large white mug and held the coffee sachet out in front of me. It definitely looked like there was already a slit in there, which seemed odd, but there was no time to contemplate such things... I raised a sharp, dirty fingernail and slit the sachet open. The powdery brown substance fell to the base of the mug. In a few more minutes I would have consumed it... I didn't want to, but there was nothing I could do to stop myself. I'd reached the coffee machine, but as I opened the lid...

What's this?

"I was right!" I shouted out loud, triumphantly. I hadn't managed to make it work before, and now I could see why. "They did sabotage it..." The entire of the coffee machine's interior was empty, having been removed as a precaution against me. That last transcript was slowly starting to make sense.

You remembered that last transcript? How?

You shouldn't mess with someone with an imagination, X. You should never have taken control of my book, letting us switch places like that.

Fool. You think that coffee machine was the only way to boil up some water on this ship? You and I both know there's another way.

No... no, there isn't another way, X. I'm sure of it. You can't make me do this... no... no you can't...

But now I was standing in the corridor, facing the pool of boiling water that had been streaming from the leaking pipe ever since my fight with Travis. I had completely lost control of my arms... In one hand I was still holding the mug with the coffee powder still at the base. In the other, a measuring jug.

"Please don't do this," I begged both X and my own hands to stop, but it was too late. I held the jug over the steaming pool, grimacing as my hand starting to burn. It hurt but I couldn't pull my hand away, no matter how hard I tried. The jug went down and scooped up about a quarter of a litre of boiling water. It burned like hell. I couldn't fight it… I poured the water straight into the coffee mug and it instantly turned a dark cloudy brown.

Yes. That's right. Now, stir! Stir!

I didn't have a spoon with me so I was using my own finger, feeling hopeless as the hot fluid burnt through my flesh against my will. I was walking back to the common room now, frantically stirring the hellishly dark drink which was turning blacker and blacker by the second. If only I could find some way to make myself trip up, like I'd been so good at doing by accident in the past. I had to find a way to spill it…

You think I don't plan for these things? I'll make sure you watch your step.

I was inadvertently tiptoeing more carefully than ever before, and there weren't any more obstacles in the way – I cursed as I remembered having cleared away all the junk from around the ship just a few hours earlier during my OCD tidying-up phase – no doubt another episode that X had a pivotal role in.

Back in the common room, I was standing, fittingly, by the coffee table. The asteroid was back, and seemed to be making its final approach. It was so close now, I could feel the entire ship shaking…

The asteroid was so close it was catching all of the light of the ship and turning bright white. Getting larger and larger, the illuminated rock had completely inverted the usual black canvas I was used to seeing through the window. Filling the entirety of my peripheral vision, I stared bleakly into the light. It seemed familiar. I knew this was going to be my death.

I raised the mug. There was no use even trying to find a way out. I had sacrificed my entire body to X. I knew now what the asteroid signified.

I looked down. The coffee had taken on a ghoulish shape in my eyes, like a demonic spectre. It was as if a mouth was forming, cackling with evil and drooling with malevolence. It was fixated on me, and its lips were parsed to form its final words.

Knock knock...

The moment had come. I touched the mug against my mouth and tipped it back. In three large gulps, it was all over.

Who's There?

Right.

Interesting.

Not dead then.

X was wrong. About a great many things, as it turned out. As I stood against the backdrop of the white light pouring into my soul, gulping down the coffee, I would have almost believed that X had it in for me. But there was something he'd missed. Something so simple, so basic, that it could only have been picked up on by close examination of one's own senses. Why WAS there a tear in the coffee sachet before I opened it? Oh yes, X had missed something quite significant. An old schoolboy trick, right there slap bang in his metaphorical face: The old switcheroo. Travis mentioned he was looking for an alternate means of distribution. That wasn't the coffee I'd just consumed. It was the cure.

No asteroid. No imminent death. Just silence. I felt an enormous wave of realisation move over me… that sudden sense of epiphany that Bob had mentioned the cure would provide. Oh boy, was that one fine drink.

Thousands of years it had taken for Bob to come up with the ultimate cure. It didn't matter that he'd had his memory wiped and didn't know he was doing it, he'd been programmed to work obliviously – a tiny little subroutine toiling away. Was all that food really purple for no reason? He'd been preparing for this moment for generations. It was all there in the food, the antibodies he'd placed had been fighting away, suppressing the parasitic disease growing inside me, but not outright destroying it. We needed an extra kick, the final piece of the puzzle, the last key to defeating X. Hence the cigarette. Unfortunately as we've established I hadn't really given smoking that thing much of a chance. Something had to change, and there was only one person who could help.

Emma. Complete psychotic maniac. But if there's one thing I'm certain of, it's that she could sure as hell pick up on the subtleties. A twitch of the eyelids... a shaking arm... just a headache, I'd say, to begin with. To some it may have first appeared that I was simply delusional, angry, tired, depressed or, later on, just flat out insane. No, it was Emma who realised something was corrupting me, turning me against my will. It was even more clear to her that this coffee obsession of mine was more than just an obsession, indeed, what with it turning out to be the drive of a mad, all-consuming parasite thriving on the stuff. She and Travis had this planned for a while...

I'd lost the coffee sachet by the bookshelves; as I suspected, right where Dom had tackled me to the ground when he was play-fighting with Wiggy and Beardy. With my cold-hearted reluctance to smoke the cure and grim determination to get my caffeine fix, the solution was ingenious. She knew that getting me to take the cure would be a fool's errand. I don't know how much of a time window there had been, but Emma had known that Travis had the cigarette; they found an opportunity to carefully slice open the sachet, unravel the cigarette and switch the contents.

Of course I hadn't noticed the last minute switch. It was crucial that I didn't, lest X catch wind of the fact that the last remnants of the deadly caffeine were now but a sprinkling of atoms floating across space. I'd thrown that cigarette out of the airlock myself, under X's control, thinking it was the cure. What was I really going to have thought of a tiny rip in the sachet packaging? Certainly not that someone had secretly taken the opportunity to swap its contents out for something with even more of a kick.

I stood staring through the window at the empty void where just moments earlier I'd been hallucinating my demise. Of course there never had been an asteroid – except for the one X had arrived on in the first place, such a long, long time ago. Of course I don't even need to still be writing this book now that I know it's not even a book - just the rambling thoughts of a man who was losing his grip on reality. That grip was finally returning. I found myself at long last feeling like I was really alive. I felt like me.

Poor Travis… whether intentional or not, he'd devoted his life to trying to save me from X. There was no getting away from that. Yet in the end, his desire had been fulfilled. X was no more. It was finally over.

So the cure had done wonders for my powers of deduction, I realised, having figured out all of the above in just the few short seconds as the bitter aftertaste of the drink ricocheted across my throat. But even that couldn't have prepared me for my next sight…

Emma was there, standing right behind me. I dropped the mug in shock. I wasn't hallucinating any more… it was really her.

"Joe?" she asked, nervously.

"Emma…" I replied, taking a deep breath. "You're still here? I thought you left with the others."

Emma was struggling for words.

"I… I chose not to. How… do you feel?" She asked, finally.

"Better now…" I rubbed my eyes. "Much better."

"I've been too scared to approach you," Emma wheezed. "You were running around, going crazy and I…"

"It's over," I replied. "We won."

"Joe, you've got to know what I did… That coffee was really-"

"I know. Remember what Bob said? He said one of the side effects of the cure was the sudden realisation of great truth." I said.

"You… figured out the switch?"

"That's not all…" I swiftly pulled Emma into a tight embrace and leaned forwards. Our lips locked together almost instantly, and we closed our eyes, kissing with all our pent-up energy. A powerful, raw and sensational feeling surged through me as we were finally able to enjoy a moment of peace amongst all the chaos and violence and…

Slap! Right across the face. So much for that moment.

"Okay, I did not see that coming," I muttered.

"This has been a complete fucking nightmare, you know!" Emma shouted.

"Of course…" I rubbed my cheek. "I'm aware of that. It got a bit messy, back there." But Emma leaned in, ready to kiss me back. I closed my eyes.

"Oh no…" Emma said, defeated. She pulled back, mouth still hanging open but with an expression of terror now on her face.

"What is it?" I asked.

"You're bleeding," Emma said faintly. I instinctively went to feel the top of my head but I noticed Emma had blood, my blood, on her front from where I'd leaned in and pressed my body against hers. As I looked down in utter despair, I noticed that my entire chest region was soaked in blood.

"Oh, no, no, no this isn't right – this can't be right, that was supposed to have been an illusion! Not real!" I yelled. Those knife games with X… I thought none of them had been real, but this wound clearly was. As soon as I touched it, I collapsed in pain. So that part of X's game –stabbing myself in the chest – that had really happened… X had covered it up – he'd only ever needed me alive long enough for me to drink the coffee. The pain had been masked briefly by the power of the drink I'd just consumed, but now it had finally hit me. I was in agony.

"What do I do?" asked Emma, panicking and trying to put pressure on my wound as I writhed around on the floor.

"No, that's not helping," I cried, pulling myself up slowly. Emma leapt up and ran across the room, quicker than I'd ever seen her move.

"We've got to find something to control the bleeding," she said, anguished, darting towards the corridor. I followed, slowly, my balance starting to falter, leaning on the walls and stumbling around corners. I was balanced about as well as I had been on my first ever wander out from the cryo room. This time, there would be no craving for caffeine. Just the simple urge to survive. I couldn't die now… not now that I was finally myself. Emma returned to me and took my arm.

The next thing I knew we were in the kitchen. Emma had made me a tightly wrapped bandage using layers upon layers of tissues from the bathroom, wrapped in straps of material from around the ship and pieces of clothing.

"That's the best I can do… I'm sorry there's nothing for the pain…" Emma whimpered.

"I think it's going to hold, for now." I croaked, feeling the weight of the makeshift bandage. "Thank you, Emma. Saving my life twice in one day, that's quite the achievement." I turned away for a coughing fit.

"Are you ok?" Emma asked.

"Yeah…" I lied, discretely wiping away the blood I'd just coughed up. I could tell the bandage wasn't going to hold, but I didn't want to admit it.

"So come on then. Why did you stay behind, really?" I asked. Emma was in tears.

"Somebody had to. The escape pod was closing, and I saw you walk away… Even with what you'd done, I knew that I couldn't… I couldn't leave you in that state. I jumped out just as it was about to launch."

"You could have gone…" I paused for another coughing fit. "With Dom and Chloe. You could have had a chance."

"I don't want that, you know I don't want that…" Emma sobbed. "You know that there's no future for me out there…"

"I said that to someone once… I was wrong…" I replied.

There was a loud beep, followed by a voice I couldn't quite believe I was hearing.

"Mr. Joe, Miss Emma, do you come in?"

"It can't be…" Emma cried.

"I am contacting you on the ship's intercom system," Bob said, his voice distorted and static-ridden. "Mr. Joe, I'm glad to detect your symptoms of insanity are audibly subsiding. It also appears that many of my own systems have been re-engaged…"

"Bob… You're alive? Where are you?" I called out in disbelief.

"A few minutes after you threw my partially disabled self through the common room window, my homing system locked onto the nearest magnetic source – the luxury escape pod. I am currently hitching a ride on its exterior shell, yet I am still in range for audio communication. The escape pod does not currently have an assigned destination, but I believe I am able to adjust its trajectory. Do you require assistance?"

"No assigned destination?" I mumbled. Dom and Chloe were on a direct course to nowhere.

"Joe… This is your chance – you knew that pod was never bound for Earth - Bob can bring it back to save you!" Emma looked at me wide-eyed. It didn't seem very likely. She must have known the pod wouldn't be able to make it back in time. I was clutching my stomach – blood had already begun to leak out again, but I didn't want her to see.

"Bob, can you do something for me?" I asked. At long last, with X out of my mind, this was my chance to do something right. A little something extra I picked up from the cure. Something lost down the back of the sofa of my mind…

"I know the signcode for Earth."

"The what now? Joe do you mean…" Emma went even wider-eyed. I quickly hushed her and spoke the entire signcode sequence out loud, all twenty or so characters, reciting it from my long-suppressed memory. We finally knew where Earth was. It was no longer a dream.

"Bob, I want you to fly this escape pod back here. Rescue Emma…" I clutched her hand tightly. "Then take the pod back to Earth, to a fresh start. Leave me…"

"No! Joe! We've come too far. We have to rescue you!" Emma yelled.

"Mr. Joe, I am afraid that in your current condition, I will be unable to provide any medical assistance. You will unfortunately die of blood loss in approximately…"

"Noooo!" Emma wailed.

"Listen to me… listen to me, Emma. There's one seat left in the escape pod." I held her face tightly. "You have to take it. Bob, save her…"

"Affirma-"

"If you're staying here then I'm staying too!" Emma cried.

"Emma!" I yelled.

"Miss Emma… I am almost… out of range… please confirm… my objectives," Bob's voice was breaking up.

"Bob, please save E… Argh!" I cringed in pain, unable to finish my sentence.

"Bob, fly the escape pod straight to Earth. Give Dom and Chloe their lives back…" Emma sobbed.

"Aff…ative. Adjusting escape pod trajectory to Earth signcode destination. Pod now entering hibernation mode. Farewell my friends… It was… pleasure… knowing… y…" Bob cut off. That was it. The deed was done. We'd saved Dom and Chloe, finally solidifying their return to Earth, but at what cost?

"Emma, what have you done?" I wheezed.

"It's what I want. I won't leave you now," Emma sighed.

"Psycho…" I muttered, jokingly. Emma chuckled. I reached over and held her in my arms. For a few moments we sat there in utter silence. What more could be done? My breathing was getting worse. I was trying to regulate it but slowly and surely it was fading. I came to a grim realisation.

"Emma… You heard what Bob said. I'm not going to last much longer."

"Don't say that…" Emma gasped, looking down at my bandaged stomach, which had become a leaking mass of crimson once again.

"It's alright," my voice was starting to crack. "You did the best you could... with limited resources..." I choked.

"Save your breath," Emma said, trying to support my wheezing body in her arms. I coughed up more blood.

"Look at me," I pointed weakly at the bloody mess on my chest. "I'm going to die. We can't change that."

"There must be something, there must be a way," Emma shook her head, too devastated to look. "I've worked too hard at this for you to just die on me all of a sudden."

"Emma..." I tried to gather my thoughts. "It's not too late for you, you can still change your mind... go to the airlock room, I don't know, find some extra transmitters or something, you can call back Bob, you can still go with them."

"Don't be silly..."

"Emma..."

"I have to save you."

"I'm dying. You have to go. There isn't another way."

"Yes there is," Emma breathed hard and took my hand. "There is."

Wearily, I found myself being led back down the corridor one last time. My eyes were half-closed, but the familiar whirring sound let me know exactly where I was – back where it all started. I leaned against one of the cryo pods, looking down, blood dripping from my chest, as I heard the clicking sound of Emma turning the dial.

"How far are you going to set it?" I asked.

"As far as it will go," Emma replied.

I smiled weakly. Any moment now my body was going to give way, but I still just about had the energy to pull myself in. Ah, the old cramped pod, how I'd missed it. I closed my eyes. This was it...

Hang on, what was that? The sound of another dial being turned... I opened my eyes.

"We go together," Emma whispered.

This time, I wasn't going to stop her. Emma was climbing into the pod opposite me- she looked over with a broad smile across her face. The pods were closing. I reached out with my hand pressed against the glass- Emma did the same with hers.

"This is what I want," she said, happily. A few moments passed.

"Emma… Can you still hear me?"

"Yes I can."

"Dom and Chloe. I wonder if they'll be happy…" I thought aloud.

"Yeah, I think they will…" Emma replied.

"They'll be alright… They're always alright…"

We had moments left until the freezing process kicked in. There was no way of knowing whether I was going to survive this or not… but there was one final thing in the back of my mind, one final detail that the cure must have made me aware of.

"Emma… I remember who I am." I said.

"Joe." Emma said. "Your name is Joe."

"No. My real name… it's…"

"Joe. That's who you are right now."

"You're right…" I smiled. "You know what? Screw the other guy."

We laughed as the pods grew louder. The glass in front of my face was beginning to glaze over in a cloud of ice. Emma turned to face me for one final moment.

"I always had you down as more of a 'Jack', to be honest."

"Well, there's always next time."

30913264R00134

Printed in Poland
by Amazon Fulfillment
Poland Sp. z o.o., Wrocław